AuthorHouse™
1663 Liberty Drive
Bloomington, IN 47403
www.authorhouse.com
Phone: 1 (800) 839-8640

Published by AuthorHouse: 08/11/2015

ISBN: 978-1-5049-2692-8 (sc)
ISBN: 978-1-5049-2693-5 (e)

Library of Congress Control Number: 2015912587

Print information available on the last page.

Any people depicted in stock imagery provided by Thinkstock are models,
and such images are being used for illustrative purposes only.
Certain stock imagery © Thinkstock.

This book is printed on acid-free paper.

Because of the dynamic nature of the Internet, any web addresses or links contained in this book may have changed
since publication and may no longer be valid. The views expressed in this work are solely those of the author and do not
necessarily reflect the views of the publisher, and the publisher hereby disclaims any responsibility for them.

authorHOUSE®

To my grandmother, who helped me through life and inspired me.

Chapter 1

High School and Me

High school is something that every teenager will have to go through once in his or her life. It is a memorable experience for every young adult to face the challenges that may come upon him or her in the world. This is exactly what I have learned in my freshman year at New Haltom Charter High School. Welcome to my confused, upsetting, and miserable teenage life. My name is Victoria Morton, but all my friends call me Tory. In my high school, I am completely ignored, as if I am a ghost walking through a wall. I am treated like a fly that just flew by that nobody seemed to care about or notice. Why? I have absolutely no idea. I think it is mainly because I just don't seem to click with certain people.

In every high school, there is always a group of friends you hang out with. But there were no friends for me. My school was like a jungle—monkeys hung out with monkeys, tigers hung out with tigers, and birds hung out with birds. The school was like Animal Planet, but I think even animals get along much better than my schoolmates got along with each other. It was as though if you were a monkey, you just would not even look at a tiger. It was just wrong to look at anything that was not your species.

In *The Lion King*, all the animals seemed to get along. Not in my school. There, it was like World War II. To survive a war, you need guns to fight for your freedom. But to survive my school, all you needed was a little bit of attitude. Wait! I take that back. You needed a lot of attitude. Attitude was the only way to survive the war of high school. If you could not stand up for yourself, you would be a doormat who got walked over every day. If you were a quiet sweetheart, you would be considered a goody-goody and would be taken advantage of.

As for me, I really did not know what, or even who, I was. I did not know who to be or even whom I fit in with. I did not want to be fake or a pretender waiting for someone to accept me in this world. I just wanted to feel confident within. I wanted a friend to be there for me all the time and stick by my side.

A friend was one of the hardest things to find in high school, probably because people were always looking for someone to respect and accept them, even if it meant changing every little thing about them just to fit in. They didn't care whether they were unhappy with the people they called friends, as long as they were with someone to make them feel complete, even if they felt empty inside.

I did not want that; I didn't need to be with a group of friends to be complete. I, Victoria Morton, wanted to be my own person. My mother always told me, "Never be a follower. Always be a leader." Gee! How many times do I have to hear the pathetic speeches over and over again? Another quote that all parents are famous for is "If everyone was jumping off a bridge, would you do the same?" Why must parents use these ridiculous sayings to get their points across? They can't just let us kids do whatever we want. Some of us might be a little more responsible than they think we are.

In this world, it is really hard to be your own person—perhaps, I think, because we are surrounded by so much temptation. We are surrounded by people making fun of us just because we look or dress differently. Some of us just don't fit the right profile. I am one of those girls who has experienced too much of this in just one year of high school.

People have always seen things in the shallowest manner imaginable, especially in high school. If you're too fat or too skinny, you are immediately criticized because you are not the perfect shape. If you are too tall or too short, there are certain things people feel you shouldn't do. But in this world of ours, people can never break their shallow feelings. If we didn't always knock each other down because of our image, wouldn't we all rise up and be happy?

I guess it's too bad that many can't see things from my perspective. Sometimes I lie in bed and wonder why people can't accept that we are all built differently. I think this is why my school is segregated the way it is.

At New Haltom Charter High School, we have groups. One group is called the Latina Gurl Crew. The Latinas always stuck together. They were Sarah, Liza M., and Letta. It did not matter who you were; if you were a Latina, you had to fit in perfectly with them.

Sarah had the worst attitude. If you wanted an example of someone with attitude, she was a perfect specimen. Liza M. was the same, but her attitude was ten times worse. I think that was the main reason she and Sarah were such great friends. If you were to walk into my school and look at the Latina Gurl Crew, you would always see those two *chicas* together. Everything they said had a don't-mess-with-me attitude. Even if you just said hello, you would hear attitude just in the tone of their reply. They looked alike, talked alike, dressed alike, and even had the same attitude.

As for Letta, she was a very quiet girl, at least on the outside. She had dyed her hair pink. She was a pretty cool girl, but that pink hair really needed to go. She was nice to me at first, but after a while she kind of annoyed me, mainly because everyone else seemed to laugh at me. Letta was definitely one of those girls who just wanted to fit in. Sarah and Liza M. were always so mean to her. No matter how cruel the others were, Letta always found a way to suck up, because she knew it was better to be cool with the Latinas while also hating life than to not be in it at all.

The next clique was the Hoodys. They were my main enemies; if I saw them coming, I would start running. The leader of the group was Kaseena, who disliked me with a passion. She looked like the Hulk, the girl was so gigantic; all she needed was some green skin. I felt that if I even stared at her, she would probably step on me. In school she ran behind me, asking what time I would like to get beaten up. I would just walk away as if I hadn't heard her, and people would always say what a punk I was. What could I do? I was not much of a fighter, and one fight in this school meant expulsion.

The Hulk's best friend was Lyka. She hated me because the Hulk hated me. It was like, if one person was against you and they had ten friends, all ten of their friends would hate you. It was just the way it went. As they would say, "You gotta stick wit' yo' peepos." Lyka would always laugh at how ugly my hair was. She once said that my ponytail was so long that one day she would sneak behind me and cut it off. Ever since that day, I haven't let my hair down; I always wear it in a bun. What if she had really done that to me? What would I have done? What could I do? This girl was just as crazy as the Hulk.

The rest of the Hoody crew were Mia and Mila; they were only nice to me when Hulk and Lyka were not around. Just as I said, everyone just needed a clique. Mia and Mila were both a little chunky. If life were *The Lion King*, they would definitely play two chunky monkeys.

Another Hoody was Rashly, who should be in a mental institution because she was way too crazy. It would take five hundred doctors studying day and night just to calm her down or figure out what was going on in that twisted mind of hers. Who knows why the girl was so crazy. All I knew about her was that she needed to be sedated. Rashly was one of the newest students in the school. It did not take much time for her to find whom to fit in with. If you were wild like a beast, the people you would get along with were the Hoodys. Rashly spoke to me only when she felt it was necessary. I mean, we weren't anywhere close to being friends, but we got along okay. Rashly was definitely a wild monkey that needed to be locked in a cage. With this clique, the most upsetting moments were not the nasty things they said, but the nasty things they did.

Every morning when it was time to go to the lockers and get prepared for class, these girls would always do something stupid. What they did was called "Hoodys rule school," or HRS. They would go around pulling pranks on every student they did not like. A few weeks ago, they filled my locker with worms. Worms were in my textbooks and notebooks.

I was first on the Hoodys kill list. What could I do? Whom could I tell? I mean, what would you do? I was the first person on the Hoodys' list, but no one said I was the last.

There was one person that the Hulk disliked much more than me. Her name was Kantar, and boy, was she annoying. Kantar had the squeakiest voice; it would get under your skin. At lunch during fourth period in the cafeteria, she and the Hulk had had a screaming battle. The Hulk said, "Everybody raise your hand high in the air if you hate Kantar." The whole cafeteria raised their hands really high and burst out in laughter. All Kantar could do was run to the bathroom, crying her eyes out.

But Kantar was kind of annoying; some teachers could not even stand her. As for the upper classmen, when they saw her coming they would run the other way. That's not the only thing they had done to poor Kantar. In gym class the Hoodys threw all of the balls in the gym at her. When Mr. Toughneck caught them, they got detention. But their only excuse was "We did not know; we thought she was the soccer ball net."

At least Mr. Toughneck gave them detention for their insane behavior. Some teachers were scared of the Hoodys; they would run from them, too. Mr. Toughneck was the kind of teacher that would enforce the rules. This is why all of the students called him Mr. Toughneck.

I know what you are thinking—why didn't I just hang out with Kantar. It was because everybody hated her, and I was not with a clique yet. It was not a good idea, as I had my own problems.

As for some of the boy groups in my school, they were the same as in any other high school. The boys were always acting as dumb as a doornail; no boy could ever mature fast enough. But no matter how dumb boys can be, girls always drool all over them, thinking they are so hot, so cute, and so "just for you." This is exactly what the Trolls were in my school. They played games with everybody all the time. Ben was the kind of boy that got straight *A*s in class, but he was as gross as ever. He ate off the floor and never took baths. Once he wanted to have the leftover sandwich on my plate at lunch. I told him, "No, go buy your own lunch." I walked to the trash and threw it away. Then, all of a sudden, he ran over there and started eating the food right out of the school garbage. When I saw this, I almost threw up my own lunch. He was the type of boy you could not go near with out smelling a bad stench. Ben was sweaty all over, and if you touched him, he was wet, as if he had just jumped in a pool. Another Troll that I could not stand was Mars, a boy that would go around pinching people to annoy them. Then he would act as if he wasn't the one doing it. He was like an annoying alien that belonged on the planet Mars. Troll number three was Dommy; Dommy was a skinny black boy that reminded me of a slinky. He looked like one of those aliens in the movie *Men in Black*. Dommy actually had a girlfriend who was pretty nice to me at school. But I was very surprised he had a girl; who would have thought that an alien could actually get with a pretty girl like her? I thought aliens dated aliens and humans dated humans. I guess it's okay to date out of your species every once in a while.

It was not that I hated Dommy. It was just that he would do the stupidest things to agitate me. He would come up to me every day after school and ask me, "Are you okay?"

I would respond, "Yes I am just fine."

"Because you look so sick, like a dog," he would reply. When he said that, it would make me want to slap him. But I would never have the courage to be as bold as some of the people in my school.

Troll number four was Mauro, who had the biggest crush on me. The whole class thought he was annoying, the teachers wished he were not a student they had to deal with. But, sadly, he was a student there that everyone had to put up with. He was a sad little person sometimes; he made Fs for grades and said they meant "funny." His glasses were never straight on his face. He wore them to the side and said it meant he was the cool one in the class. But if I were to go out with Mauro, you would never hear the end of it. The Hulk would probably scan pictures of us on Facebook or even Myspace and write the most embarrassing nasty comments ever. The Trolls never actually talked to each other, I just saw them as an annoying clique because all they did was annoy.

The other group of boys that really were the ones that would sometimes make me cringe was G-Crew. G-Crew was the clique that every boy wanted to be in. But, if you wanted to be in this clique of people, you had to be sarcastic all the time. You had to crack jokes on every person in the school, always. They weren't only class clowns; G-Crew's members were the basketball team's best players as well. I have to give it to them; they were dumb when it came to schoolwork, but on the court they certainly made up for it all.

What can I say about G-Crew? They were boys that did not have to try to find attention like the Trolls. G-Crew got enough attention just for being the star basketball players. The head of the crew was Koury; he was the person that got talked about the most. Many people say that he thought he was all that because he was the captain of the basketball team. When I asked Koury what "G-Crew" meant, he said it meant "Gangster Unit." His whole crew thought they were gangsters who should be respected by everyone in the school.

The rest of his crew was Trance, Teddy, Lyle, Zane, and Kylan. Trance was the ladies' man of the class. Every girl thought he was so cute. G-Crew teased me, just like every other crew in my high school. But Trance never did; maybe he liked me, but he never said anything. It really doesn't matter, because I had my eyes on a new guy that I thought was cute—Shawn.

Shawn was not exactly a part of G-Crew just yet, but he was on the basketball team and played well. I don't know what I thought was so cute about him. Who knows what it could have been; was it his hazel eyes, or was it his muscular body? I had the most unbelievable fantasies about him. When I looked into his eyes, it was as if I were somewhere else very special. I hoped that he would not join G-Crew or become a ladies' man like Trance. Even though he was hanging out with that particular group, that didn't mean I couldn't befriend him. However, I knew that as soon as I started to befriend him, Teddy would start to make random jokes about us dating each other. I knew Lyle, with his snakelike hair, would spread his rumors. I knew Zane and Kylan would laugh about it just to fit in with the crowd. So I thought maybe it was best to put Shawn and my fantasies on hold.

Chapter 2

More Cliques

A certain group of girls in school called themselves fabulous, trustworthy, funny, and unforgettable. I called them the Exclusive Clique of the school. They had something to talk about every day, every minute, and every second. They never hated me, but I would not say they exactly liked me either. The reason I called them the Exclusive Clique was that they couldn't exactly be classified as classy or preppy. These girls could never keep quiet; if you were a mile away from them, you could hear their conversation. If you were in China, you could hear their conversation. Every time I sat next to them in science class, I got the most ridiculous headaches you could ever imagine. In the morning, when breakfast was served at my school, they would have their own little buffet together at the back table. They each had a plate, fork, and cup, and they put a red tablecloth on the hardwood table. They even bought in candles to light.

Takeya, the leader of the group, thought she was the most precious thing on earth. She always said what she wanted to say exactly when she wanted to say it. I once saw her curse out the science teacher, Mr. Wiggles, who had gotten his name because he could never stay still for one minute. For some strange reason, he always twitched as if he were on something. As for Takeya, she ran the ghetto crew. She was one of those girls that were always wearing purses. There is not one time I have seen her with a backpack.

Her crew was just like her purse; they followed her everywhere she went, Even if it was just to the bathroom. Her crew members were Modeya, Asha, and Via, who were always two steps behind her. Modeya was her best friend; they did everything together: they shopped together, went on double dates together. Sometimes Asha went with them too, ever since she and Dommy had started dating. As for Via, she did not hate me, because I never really bothered her, but that does not mean she liked me. This girl had her days when she wanted to slap me and hug me. Once she tried to slap me because I somehow made her mad. Then the next day, she came up behind me and put her arms around my shoulders and said, "Cheer up, girl; it's such a nice day out." I don't know if the girl was bipolar or had just hit her head, but that day she seemed to like me.

Right across from them sat the Quiet Girls; they were the clique that did not speak to anyone but each other. It was not possible for them to fight with anybody or pick on anybody. The four always stayed quiet; they were loud only around each other. There was Daisy W., who was always insecure, mainly because of her weight. She was always nice to me her and the rest of her quiet friends. Her friends were Ann, Neddle, Dana, and Lita. Ann was the most annoying girl, in my eyes. She was really quiet, but every time I wanted to become close with the quiet girls, she would always find a way to make me go away. Ann also wrecked Neddle's and my relationship. Neddle and I always used to hang out, but all of a sudden Ann came into the picture and slowly started to push me away from the Quiet Girls. The way she did it was so sneaky that no one would even notice. As for Neddle, she never even recognized that I was getting left behind. Before I knew it, our relationship had vanished into thin air. It was as if we had never been friends.

The rest of the Quiet Girls, Dana and Lita, they were nice enough to me. Dana was your everyday sweet innocent girl that always got attention. I can't understand why she was liked or never picked on. The girl had big bug eyes and huge, pushed-out lips like a duck's. Lita was one of her good friends, and she always tried to get smart with people; I could not understand why she was in the Quiet Girls crew. To me she had a lot of mouth that sometimes got really weird. But the Quiet Girls still hung out with her—though for what reason, I don't understand.

The Quiet Girls also talked to the Three Musketeers. They were two different cliques that talked just to talk. The Three Musketeers were Jule, Tamy, and Zayla. Jule was the kind of girl that got straight As, but the thing that really bothered me about her was that she never studied. The girl never picked up a book to find the answer to anything. I guess the answer would just pop up in her brain. I have to work extra hard to get good grades, and yet I am still not an A student. Sometimes you just can't explain the things that happen to go on in this world. I guess in life there is always that one person you want to be like, or get what they get, have what they have. But it never works that way; some will have more, and some will have less. Either way, you're still very blessed. At least that's what my grandmother would say when I told her about something I wanted that someone else had. Jule and I weren't friends, but we were okay.

Zayla was Jules's best friend; she was an okay person to me. During our freshman year we had our little feuds that I never would forgive her for. Zayla used to always try to befriend the Exclusive Clique, because she thought they were cool. But they always used to bully her, so she began hanging out with Jule and Tamy. That's really how they became the Three Musketeers; one got booted out of a group and went into another that just took them in.

The Three Musketeers always sat across from the Peanut Heads, who were mighty agitating. Kel was an annoying boy who just happened to be as tall as the Statue of Liberty and as dumb as a … well, I don't know what. The boy had the biggest head; his head was just like a balloon. He had a big head, and nothing but air was in it. The peanuts were not always nice to me; for some reason they thought I was weird. The rest of the peanuts were Danny, Jaye, and Kaon. Danny and I talked only if his friends weren't around. Everyone called Jaye "Stretch" because he was so tall. As for Kaon, he was very conceited, and he was not even that good looking. He walked around with a comb and brush in his pocket. Every time he walked, it looked like he had a broken leg or something. Kaon was a boy that you never stopped looking at and wondering if there was something wrong with him. The We Rule Girls didn't even speak to him much, because he was more conceited then they were.

Star was the leader of the We Rule Girls; she was so enthusiastic and weird at the same time. Her hair always looked a little crazy, as if she had just walked out of a fire. Her hair was red and black and looked like porcupine quills sticking out of the middle of her head. Every time she went a little crazy, she would rub her head really hard and start screaming. Her friends were Rya, Jada, and Glow. Rya was really weird toward me sometimes. The girl made fun of me from time to time. At least Star was not a follower and was usually nice to me. Jada always was such a doll to everyone; she walked around giving hugs to people she did not like. The We Rule Girl one had to beware of was Glow. This was one person I could not stand for even one minute. Out of all the people in my class, she was the one I despised the most. A lot of people talked about her a lot, but only behind her back. Even the Hoodys had negative things to say about her, and they were her friends. I would describe this character for you, but you just might go to bed having too many nightmares. If you would like to picture her, just picture a bald man with scary nails.

Those were the crews I needed to stay away from. There was a new group in the school that had just come together. People said they were cute, happy, and perfect for each other. But, as for me, I called them Da Couples. Kadence and Lawrence just started going out at the beginning of the year. They said they were just boyfriend and girlfriend, but I really thought they were married. They act like a married couple that needed a quick divorce. Then there was Patience and Joey, who were so cute together. But they happened to start hanging out and eating lunch and dinner with Kadence and Lawrence. I guess married couples do things like that together.

Those were all the cliques in my school that always ignored me. But my question was, where did I fit in with these groups of people, or would I ever? I could not fit in with the Latinas because I was not a Latina. I couldn't fit in with the Hoodys, because I was not a girl gangster. I couldn't fit in with the Trolls, because I was not weird and disgusting. I was no ghetto girl so trying to be ghetto was just out of the picture. No way could I try and be with the couples; it was not like I had anybody. Well, I won't even go on any more. Thinking about school has given me so many headaches it's crazy.

Chapter 3

How Cruel

If you are wondering what an ordinary day is like for me, don't wonder! It is the most annoying day a teen could ever have. I usually end up sitting by myself at lunch every day, which can get pretty lonely. There are times I wish that I were famous, because I have always felt that maybe people would have more respect for me. Well, I definitely would have to worry about the paparazzi and everything. But at least I would feel like someone important. I wish life were like a dream when something is just going so wrong and I don't want it to happen. All I would have to do would be wake up, and the problem I had would be gone forever. Its not like I never tried with people at my school; I always tried to talk to someone. For example, I always tried to be Glow's friend. But every time I tried to sit next to her at lunch, she would look me up and down and say, "Excuse you." It was only because she was around the We Rule Girls.

I think she was a lot nicer when she was around Kadence more. But now that Kadence has a new boyfriend, she never makes time for her other friends. I always wanted to be Kadence and Glow's friend for some reason. I think it was because I loved their clothes, hair, and even their jewelry. My mom always says, "Never force yourself on anybody." But for some reason I really wanted to be their friend.

Every time I made the effort to be their friend, they somehow tried to find a way to push me away, like one day when I was on the bus with them and I heard them talking about boyfriends. I had no idea what to say about boys. When it came to boys, I was completely clueless; like, I did not know anything. But while I was talking to them, I could at least act like I had a boyfriend. But Mrs. Kadence caught me right off the bat. She said I did not have a boyfriend and I couldn't get one even if I tried. Then she started to brag about how Lawrence bought her a necklace with his name on it. She told me that when you have a boyfriend, you don't have to buy your things; your boyfriend will just buy everything for you. She and Glow started to laugh together. Glow said that it was pathetic that I did not have one and could never get one. This is why you don't tell anybody your business. They will make the stupidest comments you have ever heard.

At least the Latinas who always sat with a group of Latinos said I could sit with them. That is, I thought that they were going to offer me a seat, but they were not. "Victoria, come here," Liza M. said. I walked over to her, shaking and yet so perplexed, because she had never really spoken to me before. At first I thought I was dreaming, but not this time; it was really happening. I walked over to her and sat down where Letta usually sat. She said, "I feel sick, come and let me throw up on you." The whole table burst out in laughter. I got up from the table with my head held down, too embarrassed to even turn around. As you can see, trying to sit with one of them at lunch was not exactly the easiest thing to do for me.

I tried to walk around the school as if nothing bothered me, thinking that something good would happen for me one day. Letta, who got bullied by the Latinas, just found another group to hang out with. But for me it was never that easy; no one wanted to really talk to me, except when they wanted to tell me a really dumb comment. Even when I tried to get along with them, I always ended up upset. For example I once asked Glow if she could pass me the juice during lunch. Glow just rolled her eyes and said no. I can't stand her; she is so rude, and the only way she will communicate with people is by rolling her eyes. I have heard some nasty remarks about her. But maybe if she were a little nicer to people, bad remarks would not be passed around.

It seemed to me that the people that were mean and cruel seemed to get along well. Liza M got along with Glow because they basically had the same type of attitude. In the bathroom, I overheard them talking one day, and I heard them say that the Hulk was wearing Capris. It was so funny; they said her legs looked as if they were tree trunks. At least I was not the only one who got made fun of in the school.

Rumor had it that ever since Sarah started to talk to the Hoodys, she and Liza M. hadn't been getting along. Liza M. told me that the Hoodys had changed Sarah. I don't know what might happen next; maybe the girls might need a replacement. It just might be me, but I am not going to get my hopes and dreams up just yet.

Chapter 4

My Best Friend Is a Boy

I was walking to the table where I usually sat by myself when I heard a deep voice behind me. "Would you like to sit with us?" a young man said. I had to look behind me, making sure he was talking to me, mainly because that's how shocked I was. It turns out it *was* me he was talking to. I walked away hesitantly as he began to look me up and down. "Are you okay?" he asked.

"Yes," I replied.

"My name is Kingston, what's yours?" he asked.

"My name is Victoria, but everyone calls me Tory," I said. I stood up, ready to walk away. But as it turned out, he would not let me.

"Please sit down!" he said. "What is the hurry?"

"Nothing," I replied. He smiled at me as if we were already friends or something. He introduced me to a kid that was sitting next to him; his name was Lennie. We started to talk, all three of us, and I have to admit I actually enjoyed talking to them.

I started to sit next to them at lunch every day. We talked about everything we thought was good about the school. We also talked about everything we hated about the school. And there were more hates than likes. Kingston hated the uniforms the most at this charter school. He said that khaki and the collared T-shirt that represented this school were not his style at all. I said that the people here were not my kind of people. Lennie thought the whole school sucked altogether. It felt so good to have somebody to talk with. I had a clique of friends to hang with. But just when you think everything in your life is okay, something always ends up happening.

Lennie came to the table really depressed one day. I did not think anything of it until he said, "Guess what, I am moving to Florida." I could not believe my ears. My best friend was moving away from here—far away.

"When, where, and why?" I asked, demanding an answer.

"My dad just got this new job," he said.

"When do you leave?" Kingston asked.

"Next week," he replied.

***

When the following week came along, Lennie was nowhere to be found. Kingston came to sit next to me at lunch; I could tell that he was really sad and mad at the same time. "Guess it's just you and me," he said with his head held down.

"Yeah," I replied.

Weeks went by, and none of us ever brought up Lennie. One day Kingston and I started to talk about class, and the unthinkable happened. I took a bite of my turkey sandwich and got mayonnaise all over my face. I started to talk, not even noticing what was on my face. Kingston noticed and got up to get a napkin. "Tory, you have mayo all over your face" he said.

"Where?" I asked, trying to wipe my face before I died of embarrassment. Kingston grabbed a napkin and tried to wipe it off for me. All of a sudden, I saw Leya staring at Kingston and me. Then all of the Exclusive Clique started to stare at us. In front of them, Kadence and Lawrence at Da Couples' table were staring too. Then they made Patience and Joey start staring. I don't think Kingston noticed it as much as I did. Maybe it was because I was so paranoid.

As I was walking to Mr. Wiggles's class, trying to think about passing the big science test, Leya came up behind me. "Hey, Mrs. Kingston," she said.

"Leya, it's Tory," I replied with attitude.

After that terrible test was over, I had to go to gym class. Dommy stood next to me. "Do you and Kingston go out?" he asked.

"No we don't," I replied.

"Yeah, right. It is all over the school that you two love each other," he said.

"Okay, okay," I said, showing no emotion at all. I wondered if Kingston was spreading rumors about me. But that just could not be true, knowing the kind of friends we were. I let that go, as I had better things to focus on.

In gym class, Mr. Toughneck was going to make us climb the robe. That was one thing everyone feared every year. It was an exercise that we did every three months so that our climbing skills would get better. I was up first, and when I started to climb, I felt fine. But the higher I got, the more scared I became. I had almost reached the top when I realized I could not go any farther. "Don't worry, maybe Kingston, your new husband, will save you," the Hulk yelled. Glow came over and splashed water all over my pants while I was hanging from the rope. Luckily, she got a detention for her rude behavior, but that did not erase my embarrassment. The whole class laughed at me and called me a flying monkey. I was so caught up in the fact that this was one of the most humiliating days of my life that I fell right off the rope. I was sure I was going to hit the ground.

When Shawn came and caught me right out of thin air, I looked into his hazel eyes and gazed a little. After all, he was my first crush. "Don't cheat on Kingston, Tory." Glow said.

I looked at the back of my gym pants and saw they were soaked. "Tory, you peed your pants," Lyka said.

I ran to the bathroom full of embarrassment. "Don't worry; Kingston will take care of it for her," Liza M. said. The class was laughing as if I did not have any feelings. The girls that had made fun of me all got demerits, but I wanted them to get more than just demerits. People never stop to think whether I have feelings or not.

Through the day I tried to forget about everything that had happened. I was so embarrassed I felt I could have died. But what, really, could I do? The best thing to do sometimes is let things go.

When the time came to leave school, I walked onto the bus as if nothing had been bothering me, even though I could hear people whispering and laughing about the incident.

When I got home, I saw a letter on the porch. It was some kind of postcard from my family out in New Jersey. My mom told me to open it and read it out loud. But I didn't feel like talking after what had happened earlier, so I just silently read it to myself. "You know, honey, your cousin Isis is coming up from New Jersey to visit," said Mom.

"Oh," I replied. I guess it is good to see family every once in a while.

"They bought you some gifts as well," said Mom. She came out carrying a big package. I opened it wondering what Isis could possibly want to give me. The girl did not even know me that well. I opened it, and inside the package was a charm bracelet for me. She had also bought some high-heeled shoes for my mom. Also in the package were some clothes for me. Isis had bought me skinny jeans, a North Face jacket, and some ballet flats. At the very bottom of the box was a jacket worth a lot of money. I looked at the price tag that she had probably forgotten to take off; it read, "$500." My first thought was that this family must be wealthy. But my second thought was, *What if Isis stole it to get me to like her or something?* I didn't think my mom had noticed the expensive prices on the gifts this family had given us.

I eventually wrote letters thanking them for giving me these wonderful gifts.

"Tory, Isis is your age, but I think she is just a couple of months older," said Mom. "I am sure you two will get along just fine when they come up to visit."

"Okay, tell me about this family, Mom," I said.

"Well, dear, she has a younger sister that I think is now eight, and an older brother that is now eighteen," said Mom. "You will meet them as well; their names are Isaac and Angel."

"Can't wait to see what they are like" I replied.

***

The next day at school, I walked in wearing the new jacket Isis had bought me. I am not the type of person that likes to be conceited, but, I have to admit I looked good. It had been a while since I had put on clothes and felt good about what I was wearing. As I walked by the Hoodys, they snickered as usual. This time the Hulk looked like a grizzly bear in her fur coat. I went into class and sat in my first period. Behind me I saw Kadence and Lawrence snuggled up together. Kadence was sucking on Lawrence's finger as if it were a lollipop. I was so grossed out I immediately changed my seat. The fact that they would do that in front of me made me sick to my stomach. I mean, they made a cute couple, but they did not have to share their affection with the world.

Kingston came right up behind me and sat right next to me. I smiled as usual, glad that he was next to me. "So what are you doing after school today?" He asked with much curiosity.

"Nothing much, just going home to do homework," I replied.

I heard a lot of shouting in the background. It was Lawrence's big mouth. "Look at the two new lovebirds!" Lawrence shouted out with excitement to Kingston and me. Then Kadence quickly started to cover his mouth. She always did that to her boyfriend when he was shouting out stupid comments. It was a good thing that she did that, because who knew what he would shout next.

"Don't let him get to you, Tory," Kingston said. "You and I both know what we are, and that's all that matters," he said anxiously.

I never knew why I let the smallest things get to me. I hated getting talked about. I never knew what was the matter with me; I let every little thing get to me. Sometimes I wished I were as strong as Kingston, because he let nothing get to him. Everything people said to him went in one ear and out the other. But I was not like that for some reason; everything people said to me was like a stake through my heart. I was really sensitive and I let every little thing get to me. When I told my parents about this, they would say one of their famous quotes. "Did you know that I am rubber and you are glue and everything you say bounces off of me and sticks to you?" They had said that ever since I was in kindergarten. Sadly, throughout my life I was always the glue. I really didn't know how to be rubber. Maybe if I were the rubber I would be a stronger, more independent person. But I know one thing for sure: it takes more time to be the rubber than the glue.

The door slammed shut and in walked Mrs. Ma-Donny. She was our English teacher, and she knew how to pile up work. "I want a two-page essay by tomorrow, and be ready to present it," she said with great urgency. I started to sweat when I heard the word "present" come out of her mouth. I was hoping that she had said "present," meaning she was going to give us all gifts. But I knew exactly what definition she was using; it was not the one I liked hearing often.

I elbowed Kingston. "What am I going to do; I can't even speak my mind, much less present," I said, frightened at my own words.

"Don't worry; you will be fine," Kingston said. He always had a way of being so cool about everything that it annoyed me. Kingston always had the same answers all the time. He never got nervous about anything, no matter what the situation was. Someone could say, "Kingston you will have to do a speech in front of the whole world and do ten backflips." He would do it without breaking a sweat or shedding a tear. He was my calm Kingston all the time!

Chapter 5

The Presentation

The presentation in a way upset everyone, not just me this time. The look on everyone's face was so confused and angry at the same time. "I know you guys are upset, but this is to prepare you for your future," Mrs. Ma-Donny said with excitement. Mrs. Ma-Donny was the English teacher that made everything we did sound super easy. She was the type that would make you feel you had done very well on an exam, when you really failed. About a month ago, when I was walking into the school, she told me that she was so proud of me. She said that I had done well on my essay on the American Revolution, and that I had a great vocabulary. I could not wait to see my great grade the next day! When she passed it back, there was my grade. Right in front of my face, there lay a 49%. It's amazing how fake teachers can be. The only thing I admired about Mrs. Ma-Donny was her enthusiastic personality. She was not the type of teacher that would take out her problems on everyone. Mrs. Ma-Donny always had a smile on her face; even though she was a little weird when it came to grades she had a way of lightening up your day.

"This essay will be about a person that you admire," she said, making it sound even easier. "Then you will have to give a speech about your person in front of the class," Mrs. Ma-Donny said with urgency. Sometimes I wish teachers could switch off with us and see our side of the hard work. They just assign, and we have to do, even when they don't even teach it right.

When school was out, the only thing I could think about was this essay. I mean really, whom did I really admire? I was not the type that went crazy over celebrities or the type that really admired anybody, really. Almost half the class was going to do the president or some other famous person. I didn't know whom else to pick, so I picked my aunt to write about. I had no idea why I would admire my aunt, but I was just going to go with the flow and write from the heart. I finished my essay just before dinner. The next thing I had to worry about was the presentation and how I would present this report to my entire no-good class. I didn't really think Mrs. Ma-Donny knew what she was doing. It didn't make any sense that she would expect us to have a presentation ready by the next day. But in life you just have to go for it, even when you don't like the rules.

When I got to school the next day, all I could think about was that I had a presentation to make. I hoped and prayed that I would not be first up. Mrs. Ma-Donny came to the front of the room. All I could hear was the clicking of her heels walking around the class. "The first person up to do their presentation is Koury," Mrs. Ma-Donny said. Koury got up out of his seat as if he was not scared a bit. He walked up there like he was the man. As soon as he reached the front of the classroom, Koury started to talk as if he were some sort of professor. "Hello, my fellow students, today I will be talking to you about Abraham Lincoln," Koury said in a deep voice. He spoke as if he were a very old preacher at a Baptist church. I could not listen to Koury talk on an on, as his new voice was so annoying. I think he was acting instead of presenting.

"Well done Koury," said Mrs. Ma-Donny when he finished. "Are there any respectful comments about how Koury could do better?"

Kantar's hand shot up high in the air, as if it were a rocket that had just blasted off. Kantar could not wait to criticize the boy. It was definitely because she and G-Crew never got along. G-Crew always had arguments with Kantar in the hallway. They would make fun of Kantar's hair and shoes. I don't know what the arguments were always about, but Koury and G-Crew always ended up in detention because of their arguments with Kantar. "I think Koury was moving around way too much while presenting. You were moving like you were some kind of snake in the grass," said Kantar with her little attitude.

The whole class burst out in laughter.

"No! I think you're confused; the only snakes I see are coming out of your hair," said Koury, making an amazing comeback.

The entire class laughed harder than ever.

"That is enough," Mrs. Ma-Donny said, interrupting. "The next person up is Rashly."

It turned out Rashly's presentation was on her mom. I could have written about my mom, but she and I don't exactly have the best relationship.

The whole time during the presentation, she kept using "umm," "like," "whatever," "so," and even "who cares." The whole presentation was about "who cares," basically.

"Great job!" Mrs. Ma-Donny said with enthusiasm. "Are there any respectful comments for Rashly?" The class remained silent for a minute. "Tory, sweetie, would you like to present next?"

"Yes ma'am," I replied as if I wanted to. I slowly walked up to the front of the class wishing that it were already over. When I finally reached the front of the room, I felt as if I were in a life-and-death situation. I looked up to the ceiling, saying to myself, "Kill me now." I felt so sick that I could have puked on the ground. "My presentation is about …" I said, stuttering. I could not allow myself more embarrassment than I had already suffered in my first year of high school.

I heard Glow snickering and saying under her breath, "Loser."

Kingston, who was sitting behind her, threw a pencil at her back so quickly that she couldn't even have caught him in the act.

Glow turned around with eagerness in her eyes, as if she wanted to slap somebody. "Whoever that was that threw that pencil, you're lucky I didn't catch you," she said, frightening the whole class.

"Glow, please step outside," Mrs. Ma-Donny said very seriously.

As soon as Glow left the room, I felt as though a big weight had been lifted off me. But I still had ten other pounds still on me, because I still had to get through the presentation. I still continued to stutter; I couldn't help it. It was how the words were flowing out of my mouth. "I think I should get a drink of water," I said, trying to escape the presentation. As I walked to exit the room, the Hulk was right by the exit. I would be safe if only I could walk by her without any problems. The Hulk always had on big, bulky sneakers. She had every color of sneakers you could ever think of. I don't think she owned any other type of shoe, including flats and flip-flops. The girl always dressed like a boy even when it was just a casual day and we weren't wearing uniforms.

She stepped out right into the middle of the classroom in her big sneakers. I continued to walk to get my drink of water, and then the unthinkable happened. The Hulk tripped me purposely; I fell right to the floor. The class burst out in laughter. By the time I looked up to prove that I knew it was the Hulk, she looked as innocent as ever; there was no way I could prove her guilty.

I got up and left the class. The bell rang, and it was time for science. Mrs. Ma-Donny pulled me back into the room. "Honey, I know that presenting can be a little hard, and there are a lot of bullies in your class; but in order to pass, you cant keep running. You will eventually have to present," she said with so much courtesy.

"I will try harder next time. Thank you for the motivation," I said, completely lying to her. When I walked into science class, I could hear people laughing at me. I just wanted school to be done with. I hoped my presentation would be better next time. And I hoped Glow and the Hulk would get theirs.

Chapter 6
Special and Important

The next morning when I walked into school, everyone was eating breakfast in the cafeteria. I liked the fact that my charter school served breakfast in the morning, but the food they served was always disgusting. A Haltom High School graduate once told me the school almost got sued for their uncooked meals. Many of the students would bring their own lunches.

When I walked over to go to my seat, I saw the ghetto girls give me a good up-and-down look. I could not help but look back at them. I saw them sipping their orange juice out of wine glasses and fixing their red tablecloth as they ate. They thought they were the most important and special. I continued to keep walking as if they weren't there. "Be careful, honey, don't trip on anything," Modeya said, making fun of me.

"Shut up," said Via, as if she really wanted to protect me. I kept walking as though I didn't hear a word they were saying.

I took a seat next to Kingston, and we started to talk about what we might do that weekend. I really needed to keep my mind off the people in the school. A Hoody walked by; this time it was Mia, the Hulk's best friend. "How was your long trip in English class yesterday?" Mia said.

Kingston looked at me with so much sympathy, feeling my embarrassment. "Pay them no mind, Tory," he said. He knew exactly what to say to me to wipe the frown off my face and put a smile on it. He always would tell me every time I frowned, "It takes more muscles to frown and fewer muscles to smile." He told me that meant that you put more pressure on yourself when you frown. But when you form a smile, the pressure goes away.

The G-Crew walked in as if they owned the place; they looked like gangsters. It was mainly because they wore their uniform pants twice as big as they should have been. You could always see their boxers. The boys always put brushes in their back pockets so they could brush their hair every five seconds. It's funny to me how fashion changes over the years. In the sixties they used to wear big Afros with combs in the hair. Now I guess it's baggy pants with brushes in the back pockets. They were boys who thought they were it—the most important and most special. "Make sure those shoelaces are tied, Tory," Koury said. "We wouldn't want you to fall again," Trance said.

The embarrassment grew and grew inside my stomach. The only thing that stopped me from thinking about it was Kingston. It feels so good to have a true friend that you know will always be there. I think that is really what a true friend is about; it is someone who will be there no matter what; they will be there to celebrate the good and to push you through the bad. As I looked across, I saw Da Couples feeding each other. Kadence was feeding Lawrence with her fork, as if he were some kind of baby. I really thought they were married. Patience was really trying to follow Kadence with her boyfriend Joey. But rumor had it Joey might just break up with Patience. The couple crew might split for good. Looked like their relationship was not that special after all.

I began talking to Kingston about the science quiz we were going to have later that day. I could not even think straight, I felt so cold. My school put the AC on high in the middle of the summer and in the wintertime. If you had summer school, you would have to wear a Haltom sweatshirt, as it was cold all the time in the school.

The bell rang, and it was time for class. When we walked into first period, it felt as if we were at the North Pole with only a swimsuit on. We took our seats for Math, ready to sit through a boring moment of algebra. I could see Kadence's face turn a little bit pink. I could see goose bumps on her arms as she shivered. "Baby, can I borrow your sweater just for today," she said, looking helplessly at Lawrence.

"Then I will be cold," he said, looking at her as if she were crazy.

Kingston laughed hard in the middle of algebra class. "That's what she calls her boyfriend," he said to me. I couldn't believe Lawrence said that to her. Kadence had the nerve to brag to me about her boyfriend who gave her everything. If that was what having a boyfriend really meant, I could definitely wait to have one.

The Trolls entered the class late, as usual. Mr. Slender entered the class looking very serious, as he always did. "Please take your seats. If you are not in your seat by the time the bell rings, you will get a tardy demerit." He began to teach on the board, boring the class to death. "What does x equal in this equation?" he asked. No one raised a hand, and when no one raises his or her hand, it's a bad sign for a teacher. I think all of them at one point or another like to play a game where they pick the person that looks least likely to know the answer. The famous thing they do is pick someone that looks as if he or she is not paying any attention. With my luck, I was his first victim. "Tory, what is the answer?" Mr. Slender asked.

"I am not sure; that's why I didn't raise my hand," I replied.

"No its not that; it's just that you suck at math," the Hulk said. Mr. Slender gave her a look that said, "You know better."

I think she deserved a harsher punishment. I actually saw him write down a demerit for her. But when she said that, I immediately completely gave up on myself. Mr. Slender helped me solve the problem step-by-step on the board. I guess it was not that bad. "Take out your notes and work through the first page of algebra problems," said Mr. Slender. I looked behind me and saw Jules flying through every problem on that page. The girl got As in every subject. It was as if she never learned; she just already knew. I guess some things are just meant for some people.

Chapter 7

Happy Birthday Tory!

October 6 is the day of my birthday. I love when my birthday comes around. It is just a day for me to get anything I please. Every year when my birthday comes around, I never feel any younger or older. I feel like I want more new things, and that makes me happy.

Beep, beep, beep. I woke up with the sound of the alarm clock very loud in my ears. I quickly turned the volume down because it was way too loud. Even though it was my birthday, that didn't mean my entire schedule was changed. I still had to do my morning school routine, because it was a school day.

When I was dressed, I walked down the stairs with a smile on my face, excited at what my parents had for me. "Morning, Mom and Dad," I said with a big smile on my face, looking for some attention.

"Happy birthday, baby," my dad said with a smile, kissing me on the forehead. I went and looked on the kitchen table. There was a big breakfast my mom had made me for my birthday. On a plate were delicious waffles, eggs, and toast.

"Happy birthday, princess," my mom said with a smile.

"Thanks for the breakfast, Mom," I replied.

When the delicious breakfast was in my stomach, I walked into the living room. Wow! Right before my eyes was a huge gift, wrapped perfectly, with the biggest bow on top. "Is that for me?" I asked, looking at my parents, hoping they would say yes.

"I don't know, is it Tory's?" Dad asked.

"Mom, please, can I open it please?" I immediately begged.

"Well, it's yours," Mom replied. I ripped the gift open so fast I just could not help myself. I was so curious to see what was in it that I didn't even read the card to see whom it was from. When I finally was done, there was a cardboard box. My dad cut it open with a knife. Inside the box was a flat-screen TV. I picked up the card and saw that it was from Isis and the Fierce family.

I looked at both of my parents, waiting for an answer. "Isis bought me this big TV?" I asked in a very curious way.

"Yes, my dad said.

"The Fierce family's mom is her cousin," my mom said.

They sure must have had a lot of money to give me a North Face jacket and now a flat-screen TV. "Are you good friends with the Fierce family, Dad?" I asked.

"No, but I sure would love to be in their family's bank account," he said.

My mom slapped him on the arm, looking at him as if he should not have said that. I glanced at the card and then at my parents. A check for $1,000 fell out of the card. I looked at my parents like, "Wow! I really have to meet this family as soon as possible." It's not every day your cousins give you that much money for your birthday. "Make sure you call them and thank them, Tory," Mom said.

"Oh, I definitely will," I replied. But I was still shocked by the check. I started to wonder whether or not they had given me the right check, even though it had my name on it. "Mom, they sure do give a lot of money for a fifteen-year-old girl's birthday," I said, still shocked by the amount.

"They do, sweetie. I tried to call and ask them why so much," she replied. "But they insisted on giving you that amount.

Wow, was my first thought. It's not every day a fifteen-year-old girl gets that much money for her birthday.

I love when special things happen on a birthday. It is the number-one day on which a person should get some special treatment. My mom actually gave me a ride to school. The ride was very relaxing and peaceful, as I didn't have to worry about the ignorant people on the bus. When I walked into the school, Kingston was holding balloons and a birthday present. The birthday balloons said exactly what I wanted them to say: "Happy Birthday Tory!" Kingston always knew what to do to make me a happy person. I walked up to him, and he opened up his arms. He always opened up his arms when he wanted a hug from me. I gave him the biggest hug ever. Mrs. Ma-Donny came up behind me and rubbed my back and said, "Happy birthday, honey." I was so happy that I was getting birthday attention from my educators.

Before I knew it, the bell rang and it was time to go to class. "Hey, birthday girls aren't supposed to go to class," Kingston said. I laughed with such enjoyment at his silliness.

"Someone's getting lucky," Mars said as he walked by.

"Thanks for the dumb comment," I replied.

Teddy walked by and gave us the type of look one gives a girl and a boy when one knows they like each other. "So you and Kingston are going out?" he asked.

"Teddy, I would pay you fifty bucks if you would shut up," said Kingston.

"Nah, I don't do strange things for change," he replied. Teddy and the G-Crew could not even speak the English language properly. That whole crew walked as though they had broken legs and spoke as though they had something in their throat. I guess that was the new thing nowadays that the boys called cool.

Kingston and I walked to class, and right down the hall came the ghetto girls. "Get at him, Tory," Takeya said with her spicy attitude, walking down the hall with her Chanel bag, her posse behind her.

"Look at all dem gifts; looks like somebody got an early wedding present," said Modeya.

I don't think the ghetto girls could speak English that well either. But they sure knew how to spread a rumor about anyone.

As the whole freshman class entered Miss Jackolantern's literature class, a silence fell over the room. We knew that once we entered this classroom, we had to be silent. This was because we knew Miss Jackolantern just did not tolerate certain things. In everyone's eyes, she was the strictest teacher—only if you had discipline issues, of course. But in my eyes she was a great teacher that knew how to teach and discipline. Her style in clothes was very different from that of the other teachers. She would wear anything that was plaid. I don't think she was the kind of person that thought about what everybody else thought. I could see that she loved being her own person. I realized that when I saw her shoes. Most teachers dress in heels for school. But not miss Jackolantern; she wore her hiking boots. All she cared about was teaching and being comfortable.

Everyone had gotten really comfortable in his or her seat, ready to hear the teacher teach. "What we will be studying today is how we can get to know characters in any book," Miss Jackolantern said in her sweet tone of voice. She always had us study characters in books. Miss Jackolantern even read stories to us, speaking just like the character in every book. If she hadn't become a teacher, she would have definitely been a famous actress. "But first I want Tory to stand up, and everybody should wish her a happy birthday," she said in a very demanding tone.

"Happy birthday, Tory," the whole class said all together.

"Boo!" the Hulk exclaimed.

Miss Jackolantern had given her the quick evil eye. The evil eye is what Miss Jackolantern gave to any student who chose to misbehave. When you saw her eyes pop right out of her head and squint like those of an animal about to jump on its prey, you knew that you had done something unacceptable that she was not going to tolerate. "Kaseena, please step outside!" She said in a very stern voice.

What on earth was the Hulk thinking? I mean gosh, I knew she hated me. But not even the dumbest person on earth would have pulled that in front of Miss Jackolantern. "Please start reading the pages that are written on the board," she said in a very calm tone. She then stepped out into the hall to talk to the tough girl.

I hate it when something happens and you can't watch the bad one get into trouble. It wasn't that I was nosy; it was just that I liked seeing her get into trouble because the way she treated others was so wrong.

After school was out, I was so happy. I could not wait to get home and see the other gifts my family had bought me. I ran inside the house looking for my dad to see if he had a gift for me. "Daddy, did you buy me anything today?" I asked in my sweet baby voice. He took out his wallet and handed me twenty dollars. I looked at the money very perplexed, because he gave me twenty bucks every two weeks. "Daddy can I please have just a little bit more? It is my birthday, and you give me twenty bucks every two weeks."

"Well, okay, save your allowance and you will have forty," he said in his deep, manly voice. Even Isis, whom I hadn't met yet, had given me a lot more. My dad was one of the cheapest parents you could ever meet. But I had enough birthday gifts for the night. Even though my father was a cheapo-deepo, I got more than enough, and I was very thankful!

Chapter 8

Happy Halloween!

"Booooooooo!" Teddy yelled out as soon as we entered the school. "Shut up, Teddy," Metta said. It was Halloween. I couldn't believe that my birthday went by that fast and it was already the end of the month. I hate it sometimes when Halloween comes around; it's just way too spooky! It also gives the kids at my school reasons to be so stupid and scarier than usual at the same time. But that never changed the fact that they were scary every day.

Everybody took their seats in the cafeteria, and they were just starting to eat their breakfast when the Hulk and her little buddies behind her came in yelling some annoying song. The Hulk and her buddies had on uniforms with graffiti all over them. The Hulk always overexaggerated everything though. She had a crazy green wig on and some funny-looking glasses. She had the nerve to make fun of things that people wore. The Hulk and the Hoodys took their seats acting as if they were the coolest clique that ever lived. "Tonight we are going to egg houses," the Hulk said with a lot of excitement. Then all the Hoodys laughed as they nodded, agreeing with the beast.

All of a sudden the Hulk looked at me with an evil glare. I quickly looked away as if I were hiding. "You'd better watch your attitude," the Hulk said with frustration.

"Whatever," I said, replying with a lot more frustration.

"Don't tempt me this early in the morning, Tory," she said.

"I didn't do anything to you," I said with such innocence.

"Are you looking for a beat down?" she asked with such confidence. As soon as those words popped out of her mouth, the entire cafeteria went dead silent. Anytime high school kids hear the words "beat down" or "fight," their heads turn around as if they are possessed or something. Before I knew it, the entire cafeteria had their eyes glued on me, as if the Hulk and I were some kind of movie. *Oh, now what on earth did I just start*, I thought to myself.

Before I knew it, Mia had approached me and said, "What did you say?" with a scary look in her eyes.

"Nothing much," I replied with hesitation in my voice. "Guess what? You are getting a serious beat down by Kaseena," she said in a very evil, scary way. I slowly got up from the table, walking away, hoping that everyone would forget about what had happened.

"Why you walking away for?" Lyka asked, trying to start a scene.

I kept walking faster as the Hoodys continued to rant and rave about the altercation that had just gone on between all of us. "Come back, punk!" Kaseena said, trying to provoke a fight. I kept walking faster until I was finally out of the cafeteria. I walked into the bathroom and just stood at the mirror and took a deep breath. The part that bugged me the most about what had just happened was that I was too frightened to defend myself.

I heard a loud noise that scared me and shook me out of the little trance I was in for a good minute. It was just the bell. I walked out of the bathroom and caught the Hoodys' eyes staring at me. I quickly walked away and into my morning class.

When first period was over, Kingston came up behind me. "Hey, where were you?" I said with curiosity. "You sure missed a lot at breakfast this morning."

"I had a doctor's appointment," Kingston replied. We started to walk to our first period English class. I explained to him what had happened not so long ago in the cafeteria. But in a way, he already knew something had gone wrong. "Let me guess, you had a little disagreement with the beast," he said as if it were an everyday thing.

"Yes, I did. The thing is, Kingston, it was not a small fight; this time the whole cafeteria watched as she and her friends tried to start something with me," I said in a very angry way. I wanted to tell him more or even let out more of the story. But as always happens when you are in the middle of a good conversation, I was interrupted.

"Please take out your worksheets and binders," Mrs. Ma-Donny said in a very rushed tone. She was one of those people who didn't want to miss a second of class time. "First up, everyone, happy Halloween. Let's get working on our essays," she said in a very calm tone. The class was very quiet and began working on the essay that would soon be graded. The only thing I could think about was getting a good grade.

Before I knew it, the bell rang really loudly. I was so into my essay that the bell scared me. Kingston walked me to my locker, and we began talking about the cafeteria incident. When we got to my locker, there was a crowd going through the halls. The halls in this high school were always crazy. When I got to my locker, Kingston stood right behind me, waiting to walk me to the next class as he always did. I noticed that the lock on my locker was open. I couldn't believe I had actually forgotten to lock my locker. I was so mad at myself for not being conscious of this. When I opened my locker, a pile of eggs came pouring down on Kingston and me. We both fell straight on our backs. I knew right away who had committed this crime—the Hoodys.

When I wiped the yolks of the broken eggs offs my eyes. I saw everybody in the hallway staring at me. I looked over to the side and saw the Hoodys laughing their heads off. Kingston was covered in egg yolks as well, but he was not as mad as I was; he did not really care at all. "One day someone will give those girls a taste of their own medicine," Kingston said with anger.

The bell rang for everybody to get into his or her classroom. The janitor came up behind Kingston and started cleaning the eggs up. "What happened?" asked the janitor in a very perplexed manner. "It's Halloween, many things will happen on this day," Kingston said in a funny way. He always had a way of bringing humor to every situation, even if it was bad.

I went to the bathroom to scrub some of the yolk off me. I could get rid of the yolk that had spilled on me, but I couldn't get rid of the anger that was buried deep inside of me. *Those girls don't need a taste of their own medicine; they need a taste of their own poison,* I thought to myself.

Boom! The bathroom door slammed behind me. "Yuck! What happened to you?" Glow said with a very careless attitude.

I started to explain to her what had happened. "I can't believe the Hoodys actually went this far," I said to glow in a very serious manner.

"Why are you telling me like I care?" she said, interrupting in a very rude way.

"You just asked me what happened," I replied.

She rolled her eyes at me and left the bathroom as if I had done something wrong to her.

I decided to go to class and act as if nothing had gone wrong. When I got there, Kingston was in his seat. I sat down slowly; I could feel everyone staring at me. People always think I am paranoid, but do you ever walk by a lot of people and think or realize that they are talking about you? Well, I do almost every day; the only thing I do is walk away.

Mrs. Jackolantern walked in five minutes late; that's the only reason I didn't get a tardy demerit. *Ooooo that was such a close one*, I thought to myself. I hoped I didn't look dirty or smell of raw egg.

Mrs. Jackolantern began teaching the class. The main lesson of the day was how to write a good essay. This teacher was one of those writing teachers that picked on everything: every grammar mistake, every spelling mistake, and every other mistake out there. The main thing she always talked about was good topic sentences for each paragraph. Mrs. Jackolantern started to talk about the subject of the next book we would be reading. She stopped right in the middle of the classroom and took a very curious glare at Kingston and me. I looked back and just stared silently at the floor. "Please open your books and start reading the first couple of pages," she said in a very perplexed tone of voice. "Tory and Kingston, please step outside."

I started to walk slowly to the door hoping she would say, "Never mind, forget about it, we will talk about it later." Before I knew it, I was standing right in front of her, looking her dead straight in her eagle eyes. *What am I going to do now?* I thought to myself.

"What on earth happened here, and why are you two covered in yolk? Mrs. Jackolantern asked with such concern.

"Good question," Kingston replied with such sarcasm. "You know, you would be amazed at the crazy things that go on in school on Halloween," he said, adding more sarcasm to the whole conversation.

"No, seriously, what happened?" Mrs. Jackolantern asked with even more concern. *Now really, what am I going to say to her?* I asked myself. "Uh, this morning before school we … we … we—"

"We ran into a group of kids that were throwing eggs at their friends, and we sort of were at the wrong place at the wrong time," Kingston interrupted in such a convincing way. Well, it was a lie that would save us a trip to the principal's office. I was glad he said it when he did, because I couldn't think of anything else.

"Well, you both are welcome to go to the nurse and get a new uniform for the day," she said with so much sympathy.

"Thank you, Mrs. Jackolantern, we should go do that now," I said as if I were in a hurry. I pushed Kingston to the side as quickly as possible. Kingston waited for Mrs. Jackolantern to turn her back, and then right then and there he burst into so much laughter. "It isn't funny! do you realize we could be in the principal's office for messy dress code?" I said in a serious way.

"So what? Who cares? She bought it," Kingston said while laughing.

The nurse gave us new uniforms; the uniforms were kind of big, though. As I walked up the hall stairs I saw the Peanuts Heads coming out of the boys' bathroom. "We heard what happened in the hallways," said Jaye.

"Good for you all, please keep walking," said Kingston.

"Yo, how you let dem Hoodys do you like that, Tory!" asked nosy Kel.

"Don't ask," I said, wanting the conversation to end. Kingston and I walked back to class as though nothing had happened.

When it was time for our next class, we walked together. When it was time for the class after that, we walked together. We both knew it would be better to just stick together for the day. Sometimes it's better to be with someone else than to be alone.

We were together until the bell rang and it was time to pack up and go home. I still had to try to finish cleaning out all the eggs in my locker. When I looked behind me, I saw Mia and Kaseena. "I hope you enjoyed your omelet," said Kaseena.

"Yum! It was great," I said sarcastically. I watched them walk right by me as though I were a ghost. I feel as if I am a ghost every day—not just on Halloween.

Chapter 9

My Halloween nightmare was over, but at the same time it had just begun again because of the staircase at Haltom High School. The staircase was steep and shaped like a spiral. I couldn't even begin to tell you how many accidents happened on this staircase. The staircase was a very dangerous staircase that didn't care who you were or what you were. If you walked on it and weren't cautious, many dangerous things could happen. When you walked toward the staircase, you would see a sign that read, "PLEASE BE CAREFUL ON STAIRCASE, AND NO ROUGHHOUSING. ANYONE WHO CHOOSES TO DISOBEY WILL RECEIVE THREE DEMERITS." The sign always said this in big bold letters; you could not miss that sign. But in my eyes the note always said, in big bold letters, "BEWARE OF STAIRS, TORY; YOU KNOW YOU WILL TRIP!" Yes, it was just my imagination, but I knew that something bad could happen one day on those stairs. Every morning, the freshmen and sophomores had to go up the stairs to get to their lockers, and sadly, I was one of them.

One particular morning, the bell rang after breakfast. I felt dizzy because I had stayed up all night watching scary movies with Kingston. I walked into the hallway and started to walk up the staircase. The Hoodys were right behind me. The Latinas were in front of me, talking about some boy. I looked to my side and saw G-Crew right beside me. The three crews that I couldn't stand were right near me. But I knew I had to make it to the top. I quickly looked behind me, hoping that the Hoodys weren't trying to do anything to me. "Get out my face Tory," said Lyka. Then the Hoodys started yelling at me from behind. *Almost to the top; just relax, Tory,* I thought to myself.

I kept trying to stay very calm. Kaseena took a banana peel and started to play with it. She threw it on the spiral staircase right in front of G-Crew. Trance, who always wore his pants five times too big for him slipped on the banana peel, not paying any attention. As soon as he slipped, I had to grab the railing to try to hold my balance. But I didn't grab it fast enough. Lyka pushed me right on the staircase, where I bumped my forehead. Trance couldn't hold his balance either; he grabbed Sarah's long hair really hard to hold him up. *Jerk!* Sarah said really loudly, screaming at the top of her lungs. "Get off of my hair!"

Kaseena pulled me by my coat to block Trance from falling on her. I couldn't move fast enough to get out the way. Trance fell right on top of me, and we went tumbling down the stairs together. I fell on my back really hard when Trance and I reached the floor. "Trance, Tory, Sarah, Kaseena, and Lyka," Mr. Slender said in a very serious tone. As soon as the five of us heard our names being called, all of us froze. Everyone who had been on the staircase was gone, so quickly.

It's funny; when trouble comes around, no one wants to be a witness or try to help out. In this school, if you were a witness or just reported a little problem, you would be considered a snitch. I slowly got up from the floor, and so did Trance. Kaseena and Lyka came down the stairs looking innocent and rolling their eyes at the same time. "What chaos did I just witness on the staircase?" said Mr. Slender.

"What you lookin' at me for?" Kaseena said. She couldn't say anything without using slang or attitude.

"Don't speak to me like that," said Mr. Slender.

"Can we please go to class now?" asked Lyka. "You're holding us up, dude!"

"I'm not holding anyone from class; I just want to know what went on."

"I fell down the stairs and fell down the stairs," said Trance. He looked so scared saying this in a repetitive way.

"Well, that's not what I saw, Trance," said Mr. Slender in a very skeptical way.

"Well isn't that a shame? I don't really care what you saw," said Trance, mimicking the exact same tone Mr. Slender had used. But the way he said it could get any adult angry. Lyka, Kaseena, and Sarah started to laugh so hard, and so did Trance. Everyone was laughing but me; I was too afraid of the consequences.

"Well, since you don't really care what I saw, you won't care if I give all of you three demerits. What does three demerits equal at Haltom High?" said Mr. Slender.

"Is that a trick question?" asked Sarah.

"It equals a detention, for all of you," said Mr. Slender.

I wanted to say something so badly, but I couldn't; the words wouldn't come out. "I don't get one, do I?" I asked, looking perplexed.

"Yes, you do. Since everyone wants to be sarcastic when I ask a question, you all will serve the detention." Mr. Slender walked away as if the conversation had never happened.

All of us quietly walked toward our first-period class, until someone had to say something smart. "You know this is all your fault, Tory," Kaseena said.

"I'm not the one who decided to put a banana on the staircase," I replied.

"I thought you liked bananas; you look just like a monkey," she said.

Lyka and everybody laughed as if that joke were really funny.

There comes a time were you just can't take it and you can't control what you are about to say. This is when emotions take over and there is nothing you can do to stop them. At this point in time, you just want to get your point across and you don't care what happens next. *Oh no, this is one of those times; it is coming up like word vomit; I can't help it.* "I think you'd better look in the mirror; the only monkey I see here is you," I said.

Trance, Lyka, and Sarah laughed hard. Kaseena gave me a deep, evil glare like that of a cheetah waiting to pounce on his prey. *Oh no, here we go again*, I thought to myself. "Well, would you look at the time. I should get going, I said," pretending I was in a hurry.

Slam! Right against the wall she slammed me. My back had collided against the wall so hard I thought I would need a back brace. Lyka kept trying to hold Kaseena back. "Don't cross the line, Tory," Kaseena said. Trance and the rest of them just stood there waiting to see a fight. No one had ever gotten that aggressive with me before. I was ready to fight back with my words, just not with my fists. I stood there helplessly with my back still pressed against the wall. I slid down and sat right were I was; the hallway was so quiet.

I wanted so much revenge. For the first time in my life, I felt that I wanted to repay everybody who had done me wrong right at that moment. I wanted to get back at someone or something without anyone knowing that it had been me. But I knew in my heart that this could only be possible with magic. I also knew there was no such thing as magic in the world. There was only a deep silence that was always there. That silence had a way of saying, "If I had stood up for myself, what really might have happened?"

***

I walked inside the house with my back aching in pain from Kaseena's brutal slam. As soon as I took my shoes off at the door, my parents were standing right in front of me. "We got a call from the school. Why did you have a detention today?" asked my mother. She looked very perplexed; I could tell she desperately wanted to know.

Where is Kingston when I need him to make up something for me? I thought to myself. I didn't know how my best friend could be so nonchalant about everything. "Well, I sort of had a little bit of staircase trouble," I said, wanting them to let it go. They followed me and kept questioning me for about five minutes.

"Don't walk away from me, Tory; we are not done with this conversation," my dad said in a very demanding tone.

"What, I am right here!" I said, very frustrated. "I'm not a Pokemon; I can't just disappear—poof!"

"You will watch your attitude, Tory; we are in no mood for the attitude today," said my mother, seemingly as frustrated as I was.

"Okay, I will stop; this conversation is over," I replied.

"It's not over until we say it's over!" my dad screamed.

I went up to my room and slammed the door. I had enough to deal with at school; the last thing I needed was to have my parents scream at me.

Ring, ring , ring! I was saved by the bell; my phone was ringing very loudly. I was so glad that phone rang when it did, because if it hadn't, my parents would have burst into my room screaming even more. I put my backpack down and just stared at the mirror in my bedroom. I felt so alone; it was as if there were no one there to talk to. It seemed that when I wasn't getting picked on at school, I was dealing with the stress of grades. When I wasn't arguing with my parents, I was in my bedroom alone, listening to an iPod. As I looked into the mirror, I just stood there thinking about me. I was a tall, young black girl looking for a place to fit into the world. For some reason I always felt that I would never be good enough for anything, mainly because I didn't fit into any cliques. My school was predominately black, so I thought I wouldn't have any trouble with the whole race thing. But maybe it wasn't that; maybe it was everyone trying to be somebody else's friend but being unable to do so without being mean to others. I stared hard and long into that mirror until I finally asked myself, "Who am I? When will I know who I truly am? When will I be able to find my true self? Why am I so afraid to conquer my battles in life or stand up for myself?"

I heard a knock at the door, so I quickly sat down at my desk. "Come in," I said, with my voice sounding extra hoarse.

"There's someone on the phone for you, Tory," my mother said. She handed me the phone. I took it from her hands hesitantly; I was really afraid to take it. I thought to myself, *Who calls me?*

"Who is it?" I whispered to my mom.

"Why don't you find out for yourself?" she whispered back.

"Hello," I said into the phone. My voice was so soft that no one could really hear me.

"Tory," a voice said on the phone. "It's Isis, your cousin from New Jersey."

My mom smiled at me and said, "Don't forget to thank her and her family for the gifts."

"I'm so happy that you called," I said in a shy tone.

"I can't wait to meet you. My parents told me so much about you," Isis said. "I even saw pictures of us in diapers."

"Oh really," I said, trying to sound interested.

"I used to live in New Hampshire, before my dad got this great job out in New York," Isis said. "I couldn't wait to talk to you; my mom wouldn't get off the phone with your mom."

At first I was happy to hear that our moms had been talking, but at the same time I was worried, because whenever my mom spoke to someone else's parent, she would ask many questions just to find a way to compare me. I hate it when I would like to keep private business to myself but I can't, mainly because my parents will get on the phone and tell all of my secrets just to start a private conversation with their friends. I started to drift off and wonder what my mom had said to Isis's mom. Isis kept talking about plans for vacation and when we could finally see each other. I kept saying yes to everything she said. At the same time I was thinking about what she looked like, what her family looked like, or if she would even like me. I just prayed that she wasn't anything like the kids at school.

"So what's your school like?" Isis said, interrupting my daydreaming.

"Uh … uh … uh, fun! I replied, completely lying through my teeth.

"At my school everybody dresses like models; there's no way you would ever catch my friends and me in anything but heels." She said this as if she were some sort of supermodel or superstar. "What kinds of things do you like at school? Are there any cute boys you really like?" she said, urging me to answer her.

"Uh … uh … uh," I said, hoping she would ask a different question.

"You must be very nervous to talk to me today; you are so hesitant on the phone," she said, sounding very concerned.

"I am just a really shy person, and I always do that when I am getting to know somebody," I said, lying through my teeth again.

"I am sort of the total opposite; I don't know when to stop talking. I am one of those people that always have to have their say," she said like some queen. "Well I guess I will see you at Thanksgiving, Tory, and I hope you will be a little more talkative," she said.

"Thanksgiving. I will see you, Isis," I said, sounding very interested to know what she was talking about.

"Yeah, your mom didn't tell you? Our family will be having dinner together this Thanksgiving," she said in a very excited way. "I really do look forward to seeing you, Tory; please don't hesitate to call," Isis said in a very demanding tone.

"I definitely won't," I said, lying through my teeth.

Chapter 10

Happy Thanksgiving

Thanksgiving is a day when all of your family comes together to celebrate friends and family. In my own opinion, I think it is just a day when you get to stuff your face as much as you want and no one can tell you when to stop eating. I was looking forward to seeing Isis this Thanksgiving; I had always wondered what she was like. I wondered how she would dress, talk, and look, and what she would think of me. But I also wondered what would happen if I finally met her and she didn't like me. What if she hated me? Well, I was already used to the criticism at school, so I had nothing to worry about if she was evil.

I was so glad it was a holiday and there was no school because of Thanksgiving. The only thing I hate about Thanksgiving is seeing family members that I really can't stand. There is always some part of something that I have to tolerate. For example, my older cousin who was coming up from London was as evil as a snake. I didn't know if she and Isis would hit it off and become best friends, and leave me out like a dog. But what could I do this Thanksgiving other than stuff myself and hope for the best?

The big dinner would be hosted at my house, so I was the one that had to help my mom get prepared. We had about thirty people coming to our house. I just hate cleaning up after people and big parties, but this was where the big dinner would happen.

"Tory, get downstairs and clean these dishes," I heard my mom yell from all the way downstairs.

"Coming, Mom," I said as if I were happy to do this.

"Tory, come sweep this floor; guests will be here any minute," my dad screamed from the living room.

"Tory, come clean this bathroom; it looks a mess," my mom yelled from the downstairs bathroom. For the next couple of hours, I was the housemaid and slave. I heard my name being shouted around the house everywhere I turned. This is the part I hate about being an only child; there is no other child there to be bugged as much as me.

"Okay, the house is all set; thank you for your assistance, Tory," my mom said with excitement.

I rolled my head up slowly and looked at her with exasperation, as if I had just climbed out of the Grand Canyon. She smiled at me, looking at me with such sympathy. I stared back with my tired eyes, looking beaten down and torn up. "Well, what are you looking at me like that for? Go get dressed," she demanded.

My mother has absolutely no sympathy for anyone. As long as everything is run her way, which is perfectly and smoothly, all will be well.

I took a nice cool shower to calm myself down and get the heat off me from the cleaning. I opened my closet door, trying to find something to wear; I couldn't find anything. The snake from London was coming any minute, and I didn't want her pulling at my clothes and judging the way I dress. Lauren Heyburn is her name; she has an English accent that my mom thinks is so great. Everything about her is so perfect; she should change her name to "Perfection." Her hair is always flawless, her dress outstanding. She could walk into a room and everybody would think she was some kind of celebrity. Lauren goes to one of the top prep schools in London and comes first in her class every year. At the same time she still manages her piano playing, violin playing, and tennis playing. There is no way I could compete with that, even if I tried.

I got dressed in my black skirt, white collared shirt, and black heels. I pinned my hair up and put my necklace an earrings on. I looked in the mirror and felt an ounce of confidence within myself.

The doorbell rang. "Tory, get down here right now and get the door please," my mom yelled, sounding happy. "I think the Hayburns are here."

I didn't even make it down the stairs fast enough. My mom was already at the door before I could get there. She opened the door, and outside was the Fierce family. My mom greeted all of them with a big hug, and so did my dad. "We thought you were the Heyburns from London at the door; we weren't expecting you this early," my mom said.

"We thought it would be a good idea to come and surprise you," replied the Fierce family's mom.

There I was, standing at the bottom of the stairs, looking at everyone greeting everyone else except me. I saw a slender, tall pretty girl look at me with suspicion and then look back at our parents greeting each other. Then I looked down and saw a young girl that looked about seven or eight smile at me. On the other side there stood a tall boy that looked about eighteen. "Oh, Tory, these are the people I have been waiting for you to meet," my mother said in a soft tone.

"These are your cousins Isis, Angel, and Isaac," Aunt Claire said in a very nice, sweet voice. Aunt Claire was the mother of the three children that stood before me. She was really thin and had long, curly hair.

"I am your uncle Roger," said a deep voice from behind Aunt Claire. He was really tall, muscular, and strong, with a deep voice that made him sounded as though he had been in the army at one point in his life.

"You kids go run along and get to know each other while the adults go talk," said my mom.

"Play nice, you four," said my dad.

I watched my parents and the Fierce family walk into the kitchen and start talking. "Do you guys have any bags you need me to help you bring upstairs?" I asked, looking scared.

"No," replied Isaac.

"We are not staying the night," said Angel in her tiny voice.

"Well why not? Isn't Jersey a bit of a drive away from New Hampshire?" I said, looking concerned.

"We can't stay because there is not enough space," Isis replied. "Aren't your other cousins staying over—the Heyburns?"

"Oh yeah," I replied, trying to seem happy about seeing them. "So where are you staying?"

"We are staying in a hotel not too far from here," Angel replied.

"Oh that's good," I said. All three of them continued to stare at me with blank faces. "Would you like to see the house?" I asked, trying to stop them from looking at me so hard.

"Sure," Isis replied with enthusiasm.

The three of them followed me upstairs; first I showed them my bedroom, which wasn't a mess, thank God! Isis came straight into the room and wandered around it slowly. "Nice place," she said with a smile on her face.

"Isaac, you are welcome to come in; you don't have to stand at the doorway," I said, trying to accommodate my new guest. He gave a great big smile and slowly walked into the room. Angel went straight to my bed to look at all the teddy bears I had. "Do you like that?" I asked, trying to make conversation.

"I have the same one at home. It is the one my mom sent to you on your eighth birthday," she said, smiling at me.

"Oh really!" I said, feeling shocked.

"Yeah! I have the same one at home; Mom gave it to me on my eighth birthday," Isis said, looking straight at the bear.

At that moment I knew I had shared a bond with these people that somehow made me really close to them; I just hadn't seen them in years, maybe because of the distance.

"I am so surprised you don't remember us visiting at every holiday when we were little I remember seeing you," Isaac said in a deep voice. I was surprised he even talked; at first when I saw him, I thought he was some kind of mute. I guess people are right when they say you should never judge a book by its cover.

"Why don't I show you the rest of the house," I said, insisting they follow me.

My house was your everyday, ordinary family house. It wasn't at all big; nothing spectacular either. I was showing these people around as if I were showing off a mansion or just having a show-and-tell game with my classmates.

"Kids, come downstairs; the Heyburns are here," my mom yelled from downstairs.

Saved by the bell, I thought to myself. I started to walk down the stairs behind Isis. I looked at her clothes and thought to myself, *Wow, I wish I could dress that fabulously.* But only in my dreams could that wish come true. She looked as if she had popped out of the magazine *Seventeen* and had her makeup professionally done by a professional makeup artist. Next to her I looked like a grandmother waiting at the sidewalk to pick up my grandchildren. As for Isaac, he looked like a famous basketball player who would be at home on posters hanging on the walls of young boys who idolized him because of his amazing talent. Then there was little Angel; she was the cutest thing. She seemed as if she could be in commercials advertising toys or maybe even clothes for some brand.

The Heyburns greeted us like family they hadn't seen in a decade. On my face I wore a smile, but I was thinking in my head, *We saw them last summer; what are the tears for?* Not even the Fierce family, who hadn't seen us in ages, had acted as if one of us had died, crying and yelling as if it were the end of the world.

Lauren quickly greeted Isis with a hug. It was very quick and fake at the same time. "It's so good to see you, Isis; you look almost as good as me, darling," she said in her English accent with a very sassy attitude.

"Good to see you too, darling," Isis replied. "You are for once not looking a bit smutty, as you did last Christmas."

It was like a cat had caught Lauren's tongue. Lauren looked at the ground as if she were embarrassed.

"What's wrong, Lauren? No comeback?" asked Angel.

"I always thought you were the cutest little thing, Angel, but please, you are so much cuter with your mouth shut," Lauren said. "Please do yourself a favor and don't take any lessons from your sister Isis."

Isaac wrapped his arm around Isis and Lauren. "Would it kill you two to get along for one second," Isaac said.

"Oh, Tory, I didn't even know you were standing right there; you could almost pass for a ghost," Lauren said in an evil way, gawking at me. "Oh, and also you're looking quite invisible; some things don't change." She pushed Isaac's arm off of her and went into the kitchen, where all the adults were engrossed in their conversation.

As she walked away, Isaac said, "at-ti-tu-ed." I couldn't believe the way Isis stood up to

Lauren. She had a way of defending herself when she knew she was in the right. Isis turned to look at me quickly. I immediately shook and didn't know what she was about to say. "Why would you sit there and let her disrespect you like that and not say anything?" Isis asked with curiosity in her voice.

"Well …" I said hesitantly, "I like to give people the cold shoulder when I feel they are being a little rude."

"Okay, just don't give her the idea that it is okay to disrespect you whenever she wants," replied Isis.

"Thanks. I will make sure I say something back next time," I said, lying through my teeth.

"Everyone gather around the table for prayer," my mom yelled from the dining room table. I followed behind Isis to the dining room, where the others were taking their seats I quickly grabbed the seat next to Isis. Isis saw me and gave me a big smile. "Please hold hands and bow your head in prayer," my mom said. As everyone began to assume the prayer position, I decided not to. I opened my eyes during the prayer to peek at my family. My mom looked at me and gave me an evil glare, letting me know I should bow my head in prayer.

As I looked down, I saw something shine in my eyes—something big and shiny! It was a big diamond on Isis's left hand. "This family really has it all," I whispered to myself.

"What's that?" my mom said curiously.

"… Uh … uh, great prayer," I replied hesitantly.

"You silly goose, we are not even done with prayer, sweetie," Aunt Claire said.

"Why don't you say a few words, Tory," my mom said insistently.

"Of course," I replied. "Thank you, God, for this wonderful meal. Thank you, God, for this wonderful family. Thank you, God, for the trees and animals. Let's eat!"

I said the prayer so fast that I don't think God heard a word I said, and if he had heard it, he would not have responded. Everyone at the table started to laugh. It went from a serious prayer to a prayer that didn't even sound like a prayer.

"Angel, would you like to say a few words?" Aunt Claire said to her daughter. Aunt Claire had the sweetest voice; you would think she was a guardian angel.

"Yes," replied angel in the cutest voice ever. "God is good. God is great. Let us thank him for our food."

Anyone would fall in love with Angel. The girl was just perfectly adorable. Her hair was in ponytails that always pulled her hair back tight enough so you could see her perfect heart-shaped face and her cute little button nose. Angel had curly bangs that hung down her forehead. She was definitely everything that someone would want in a little sister. It was too bad for me that I was an only child.

"Isis, honey would you like to say a few words?" asked aunt Claire.

"No thanks," replied Isis.

"Isis," said Aunt Claire sternly. "Pray."

"Everyone at the table said a few words; I think it's good that you do too, honey," said Uncle Roger.

Isis made a face that said, "Why must you bug me? I am so innocent and quiet." She began to speak quietly and as though she were a little annoyed. "Thank you, God, for this wonderful meal. Thank you, God, for this wonderful family. Thank you, God, for the trees and animals. Let's eat!"

I smiled at Isis; she had said the exact prayer I had said, and it meant something, because she had actually remembered it all. Everyone at the table chuckled—everyone except Lauren, that is.

"You remembered my prayer, girl," I said, chuckling.

"How could I forget the best prayer here?" Isis said.

"Looks like we have two sarcastic twin sisters at the table," my dad said.

Isis and I smiled at each other and laughed.

"I think it is just amazing that you remembered the same pathetic prayer as Tory," Lauren said in her British accent.

"I don't recall seeing or hearing you say a prayer, darling," said Angel, mimicking Lauren's accent.

Isis shot Lauren a glance that made her look as though she were going to slap her back to London.

"Please be nice girls," my dad said sternly.

"I agree with that," said Isaac.

Everyone started to eat; we all became engrossed in eating. The turkey looked so good. I almost became one of my favorite cartoon characters, Taz, and pushed it down my throat whole. But it was thanksgiving, and we all had to share.

I looked at Isis, who was eating the food off her plate and staring at Lauren. She stared at her like a savage beast ready to rip the head off of its pray. "What are you gawking at Isis," Lauren asked with attitude.

"Eat your mashed potatoes, Lauren. If you want to be mean and not be nice you shall pay the price. Swoop." Isis mumbled under her breath.

I couldn't really make out what Isis was saying, but I definitely wasn't crazy; I knew I had heard something that rhymed. I also knew that I had heard the word "swoop."

"What is swoop?" I said, accidentally out loud.

"Soup's over here, honey," my mom said immediately, interrupting my thoughts.

"Oh I didn't want soup," I said quickly. But before I said it, Isis had passed me the soup. "Why did you say 'soup'?" I whispered.

"Yes, please have some soup," Isis said, insistently.

"No, I mean why did you say, 'swoop'?" I asked her.

"Oh, because I love soup too," she replied.

Isis still hadn't answered the question; she was beating around the bush, and I was still trying to figure out what "swoop" meant. She had gotten me so confused I was saying "swoop" instead of "soup," and I couldn't put the puzzle together.

As I was thinking to myself, I stopped eating and looked around the table. *Pop, pop, pop.* I was immediately pushed out of my imagination. I looked up and saw Lauren covered in mashed potatoes. Her face was completely a mess. "What the fudge?" said my dad. My mom got out of her chair to make sure Lauren was okay. I quickly passed her a napkin to help wipe Lauren's face.

"Oh, sweetie, what happened?" My mom asked. Lauren's mom came to help her up and excuse her from the table. My mom helped and showed them to the bathroom.

Lauren began sobbing and looked embarrassed. "It all happened so fast I was just sitting there, and there were these firecracker noises on my plate, and the next thing I know, my face is covered in potatoes," Lauren yelled. I could hear her freaking out in her British accent.

I looked around the table and saw that everything had gone quiet. Then I looked at Angel. She had turned her head away from the table and started to laugh. Isaac was laughing as well. Even though I didn't care for Lauren, I still didn't laugh, as I was so shocked at how quickly the incident had happened. It just wasn't reasonable that her food would fly up into the air and become her new facial. I looked at Isis suspiciously and saw that she looked nonchalant. She looked as if nothing suspicious here had happened. I glanced down at my plate and continued eating. "You okay, Tory?" Isis asked, looking concerned.

"Yes, it just was impossible how her food got on her face," I said, trying to get an answer out of Isis.

Isis shrugged her shoulders and looked at me like "Oh well." "What comes around goes around, I guess," she said. I knew karma didn't come around that fast, and if it did for Isis, it sure never did for me with kids at school.

Lauren came back to the table. My mom and Lauren's mom sat down and continued to eat. Everyone went back to conversing. Lauren's attitude had completely changed. She wasn't giving Isis and me dirty looks, and nothing smart came out of her mouth. All went back to normal.

"Who's ready for dessert," my mom asked after a while.

We had dessert, and all went well. Everyone was soon way too full to get up from the table. My dad put some music on, and everyone danced and was having a good time—everyone except Lauren, that is. She sat there and started to pout. *I mean, it was just food that got on her face. What is she so upset about?* I asked myself.

I walked over to try to talk to her, but Isis grabbed my arm and gave me a smile. "Come dance with me, twin sister," she demanded. "I am so glad that I got to see you again and spend this holiday with you."

"Same here," I replied.

At the end of the day, everyone was exasperated. The turkey had been getting to everyone, and people just wanted to sleep. The whole family started to hug and kiss each other good-bye. "Do you want to go to the mall tomorrow with me?" Isis asked.

"Sure," I replied. I was so happy she really liked me; it felt so good to have a friend that was really there. The Fierce family left and went to their hotel. I would rather they had stayed than the Heyburns; now I had to deal with Lauren all alone.

My mom showed the Heyburns to our guest rooms. I was so tired all I wanted to do was sleep. I took a shower and then collapsed right into my bed. It had been a great Thanksgiving and I'd had a great time with Isis. I just wished she lived in New Hampshire.

The mashed potato incident was not forgotten. To everyone it was just a freaky accident, but to me it was a mystery that needed to be solved.

Chapter 11

*W*here am I? How did I appear in my school? Where is everyone? Why am I in my pajamas? I had so many questions going through my head. I was in my school with the lights shut off, standing in the middle of the hall. I didn't understand what was going on. Just the night before I was having Thanksgiving dinner with my family, and now I was in the middle of my school with no lights on and no students to be found. I was trying to think about what I should do, wondering whether I was in danger.

Suddenly the lights flicked on and my heart stopped pounding. There were students from my school running down the stairs. There were people rushing out of the cafeteria. Then there I was, standing in the middle of the hall, trying to see what everyone was running toward. Then I finally realized they were running toward me. "Stampede!" I yelled. I started running as fast as my legs could take me down the hall. I knew there were people in my school that really disliked me, but I would not let them tackle me; this time I was going to run.

I ran outside toward the field where the kids of Haltom High played their sports. I ran until I finally hit the middle of the field. I stopped, thinking maybe I was safe here. I started to breathe very heavily. *What on earth could I have done to make the whole school run after me?* I thought. More people were coming down the field to get me. I was petrified.

I ran right back around the school and back into the halls where I first started. I kept running and running and running; even some of the teachers were chasing after me. I still didn't know why the whole school was chasing me. I ran so fast that I wasn't even watching where I was going. I ran straight into the door of the janitor's room. I fell and was so dizzy from my clumsy collision. I felt as though stars were circling my head.

Then the door started to shake; the sound of it grew louder and louder. Arms popped straight out of the door; then the door grew legs. In the middle of the door grew large eyes. I tried to get up and run, but it was too late. The door picked me up and began shaking me really hard—so hard that I got dizzy and almost fainted.

***

Wake up, Tory! Wake up, Tory! When I woke up, Isis was shaking me really hard. "Girl, you were knocked out for a good minute there; for a second I thought you were dead," Isis said laughing.

"Wow! I had a weird dream," I replied, sounding completely delusional.

"What was your dream about?" Isis asked, looking concerned.

"The whole school was running after me, and I had no idea why," I said, looking scared. "Then I was being shaken by a door."

"Ah, being chased by your whole school and being shaken by a door," Isis said in a nonchalant way. "I think you watch too much TV."

"What are you doing here? I thought you left last night," I asked.

"Yes. Did you forget that we were going shopping?" Isis replied, looking at me as if I had ten heads.

"Oh, that's right," I replied.

"That dream really gave you some sort of amnesia," Isis said.

"Indeed," I replied.

"Get dressed; it is time for the mall," Isis said with excitement. I gave her a very perplexed look. "You know you want to go and get new clothes," Isis said.

"Well I guess," I said as if I were exasperated. As I started to get out of bed slowly, Isis pulled me by my arm to get up. She ran to my closet and started to pick out my clothes. "If you're looking for anything fashionable, I don't have it," I said.

"You have a lot of great clothes in here," Isis said. "But you could use some of my help. It's a good thing we are going shopping together."

"Joy," I replied.

She picked out jeans and a collared top and placed them on the bed so they wouldn't wrinkle. "Do you wear heels"? Isis asked.

"No, are you crazy? I will fall on my face," I replied.

"Well, honey, you are about to start," Isis said. "I think I have some heels in my mom's car. Good thing we drove here. Do you have any purses?"

"No, but I have backpacks," I replied.

"You're kidding, right?" Isis said, laughing to herself.

"I'm sorry I'm not a Barbie like you," I said.

"It's not about being a Barbie; it's about being a lady," she said. "Honey, you need style, you need flair," Isis said.

I sat down and listened to her as she began to preach the fashion gospel. "You have the body of a model, the physique of a goddess," she said. "Own it! Stop walking with your head held down; walk with it held high."

"But," I said.

"No buts," she replied loudly. "Why be small when you can be big? Why be less when you could be the best?" she said with enthusiasm.

"Okay, I will wear the heels," I said with exasperation in my voice."

"And?" Isis said, waiting for me to finish the sentence she wanted to hear.

"And the backpack," I said.

"It's called a purse, honey, a purse," Isis said, making sure I understood. "Now, I am going to step out and get your purse and heels, and you are going to get dressed." She left, and when she came back into the room, I was dressed and ready to get the shopping over with. She gave me some black high-heeled boots and a black leather purse. "Let your hair out, and put curls in it," she said.

"Why? I like it in a bun," I replied.

She started to pull at my hair, trying to fix it. "Where is the curling iron?" she asked.

"I don't have one," I replied, sticking my tongue out.

"Well, looks like we will have to go and find one," she said, sticking her tongue out right back at me. In less than two minutes, she came back with a very big curling iron.

"Where did you find that"? I asked.

"It doesn't matter. what matters is that I found it and we're using it," Isis replied.

She started to do my hair, making it first straight and then a little curly. I started to pray silently to myself, *Please don't burn my hair.*

"Now that we have completed the hair, it's time for the face," she said.

Isis was like the black Barbie doll I'd never had. She was really nice, and it was almost impossible to say the word "no" to her.

She grabbed the makeup out of her bag and started to put it on my face. "Remember, wherever you go, always look polished," she said.

"Yes ma'am," I replied.

When she finished dressing me up like I was her doll, I stood up and walked to the mirror and saw my reflection. I immediately scared myself and almost fell back. "Wow!" I said.

"Honey, you never looked better," Isis replied.

I walked slowly toward the mirror. I put my hands on my reflection; it was really me, the Barbie. I looked just like Isis in a way. "Am I good or what?" she said.

"It's a whole new me," I said.

"Well let's go before my mom doesn't want to drive us to the mall anymore," she said.

"Yeah, let's go," I replied.

We both walked to the door, and Isis stopped right in front of it. "Aren't you forgetting something?" she asked.

"What?" I replied. We both stood for a second and looked around. "Oh, the backpack," I said.

"It's a *purse*. If you keep calling it that, people will look at you like you're crazy," she said.

As I walked down the stairs of my house, my mom was walking around trying to straighten up the house from the thanksgiving dinner. My dad was about to leave the house. It seemed as if everyone was in his or her own world. When I walked down with Isis, both of my parents stared at me. "Who are you?" my dad asked. "And what's all this?" he said, pointing to the makeup on my face.

My mom stared at both of us blankly. "Looks like we have two Barbie dolls, not just one," my mom said.

We both walked outside to Isis's mom's car. "Mom, can you just give me a couple of bucks to go shop with Tory?" Isis asked sweetly.

I watched closely as her mom handed her about fifty bucks. "Gee, girl, I have to wait a year before I receive that kind of money from my parents," I said, looking absolutely amazed.

"You just sort of have to learn how to compromise," she said with a mischievous smile on her face. "You have so much to learn from me, love."

I strapped on my seat belt, and we drove for about nine minutes before we were finally at the mall. "We can meet here in about an hour," Isis's mom said. I watched Isis's mom walk away as we went up the escalator.

"Are you ready?" Isis asked.

"For what?" I replied.

"To change your style into mine," she said.

"I guess," I replied. "I actually have enough money. I cashed that one-thousand-dollar check you gave to me for my birthday," I said.

"Don't even spend a dime of that; everything you buy today is on me," she said.

"Well, okay … it's like you're some kind of money tree," I said.

"Yeah, but money doesn't grow on trees; it grows me," she replied.

Isis grabbed my hand and ran with me into a store. She took about ten shirts and piled them on me. I started to lose my balance and almost fell over. "Isis, are you sure we can afford all of this stuff? I mean, shouldn't we really be on a budget or something?" I said, looking intimidated by the prices.

"Don't worry about a thing; we get discounts," she replied with a smile.

Isis walked to the dressing room, and I followed. When she got to the dressing room door, I handed her the clothes to try on.

"Why are you giving the clothes to me?" she asked, looking perplexed.

"I thought you might want to try them on," I said hesitantly.

She laughed and looked at me weird. She went behind me and pushed me straight into the dressing room. "Today is about you, girl," she replied. "The mall is my palace, and you are a visitor," she said, as if she were a princess.

I tried on the first outfit. It wasn't my style, but it was Isis's. She made me come out and show her what every outfit looked like. "Never be shy; walk with confidence," she said. It was like being in a fashion show, only for once I wasn't a nobody in the crowd; I was the model, the superstar, the one that everyone looked at. I tried on every outfit she picked out, and we went running around from store to store. Every time Isis found something she liked, she had no problem taking out a credit card and buying it. Money was like candy to this girl. Life couldn't get any better.

After we had completed our little shopping spree, I was exhausted. "Is your mom going to be mad that you spent all this money on me?" I asked, looking concerned.

"No, I drop more money shopping for me; don't worry about it, Tory," she replied in a nonchalant manner.

I felt tired. My arms felt like Jell-O. I didn't feel as if I had been shopping for clothes; I felt as if I had been grocery shopping for my mom. The bags we were holding were heavy, and there were many of them. "You are turning into a mini me," Isis said.

"I definitely feel like a mini you, Isis," I replied.

"Are you hungry?" she asked.

"I am starving; shopping with you is no easy job," I replied. We went to the mall food court and ate at the ice-cream place. "We should do this again sometime," Isis said.

"Yes, we should; it was great," I replied. "It's too bad you're leaving soon; school is going to start," I said.

"Indeed, don't remind me," Isis replied.

"So where did our family members go?" I asked Isis, looking perplexed.

"Isaac went to the movies with a friend that he knows from here," Isis said. "Also Angel went to play in the park; my dad took her," said Isis.

"Well, it's good to know that they're not bored," I said. "I am so mad that you are leaving soon."

"Let's just say I won't be too far away from you, Tory," Isis replied with a little smirk on her face.

"What do you mean by that?" I asked, confused. "New Hampshire is a bit away from Jersey."

"Never mind," she said, wanting me to forget about the conversation.

As I was eating my ice cream, I stopped to look at Isis. "Can I ask you a personal question?" I asked, looking down at the table.

"You can ask me anything you want, sister," Isis replied.

"How do people treat you at your school?"

"Well, they treat me like normal, but they know that they need to respect this princess at all times," she said.

I started to laugh; she was such a queen.

"Why?" Isis asked. "How do they treat you at your school?"

"Uh," I said hesitantly. I didn't want her to know the girl I really was at school, but I didn't want to tell her any lies either. I saw pictures in my mind that were all over the place. First I saw Kaseena stuffing worms in my locker. Then I heard the harsh comments in my ear from G-Crew. I saw everyone laughing at me constantly. Then I finally said it; it was coming up like word vomit. I couldn't control the words in my mouth, and they slipped out. "I am treated like the school dog," I said with a little smirk on my face.

"You're kidding," Isis replied.

"No, girl," I said.

"May I ask why?" Isis asked in a sweet, concerned little voice, sounding just like her sister.

"It's such a long story; where do I start," I said.

Just then, Isis's cell phone rang really loudly. Isis picked it up; I sat and watched her have a short conversation with her mom. "We have to leave now; my mom is waiting for us downstairs," Isis said.

We both quickly threw away our food and grabbed our bags. As we were walking down the hall to get to the escalator, we started talking. We walked fast so we wouldn't keep Isis's mom waiting any longer than she needed to.

"You are such a hood rat," I heard loudly from up ahead of me. It sounded like someone from my school. I looked up ahead and saw the Hoodys, turn the corner. My heart started to beat so fast that I thought it would jump straight out of my body. I saw them walking directly toward Isis and me. I turned the corner and started to walk to the right, where they wouldn't see me. I had seen that they were walking with my other worst enemy, Jayla Hollens.

I couldn't even begin to tell you about Jayla. She invented the word "bad"; she was worse than bad. Jayla had been expelled from three different schools and had been to juvenile twice. Jayla was one of those people you couldn't mess with or you would be in for a scare. I think she stuck with that crew because they were all bullies. They were perfect for each other: scary, stupid, and dumb. Jayla also used to hang out a lot with the Exclusive Clique; she was a ghetto girl as well. It seemed that everyone liked her when she went to the school—before she got expelled.

The worst thing that could happen would be for them to see me here. As I was hiding, Isis kept walking, not even noticing how quickly I disappeared. "Oh, look at Miss Barbie Doll," said Kaseena.

"Who are you?" Isis asked.

The Hoodys kept walking and started laughing in their loud, ignorant voices. I waited for them to pass by, hoping they wouldn't see me.

"Tory, where are you?" Isis yelled.

I quickly jetted over to Isis, hoping the Hoodys wouldn't see me. "Shh! Are you crazy?" I said in a whisper. I grabbed her by the arm and pulled her into the corner with me.

"Tory," she whispered, "whom are you hiding from?"

"These bullies from my school that I really hate," I said softly.

"So you run?" Isis said, looking perplexed. "You know that just makes me more anxious to bother them," she said.

"Don't you dare do that!" I said, looking scared.

"Tory, they can't do anything," she replied. "You think just because they're big makes them the top dogs?"

"Yeah," I replied. "Well, what did they say to you?"

"They called me a Barbie and walked away," she replied. "I don't even care; that's a compliment. Why are you so scared of them?"

"Well, it's kind of a long story," I replied.

"I have more than enough time to hear the story," Isis said. She looked straight into my eyes, wanting to know. We walked into a store where the Hoodys were trying on boys' caps. Isis and I hid behind the coats, where they couldn't spot us.

"See the girl in the jeans? That's Jayla Hollens," I said.

"Yeah, I see the ape," Isis said.

I started to silently laugh and told her to keep her voice down. "See the girl in the sweatpants? That is my worst nightmare."

"Is that a girl or a boy?" Isis asked.

"It's a girl," I replied. "I call her the Hulk."

"Lord! I see why," Isis replied.

"The other two at the side are Mia and Lyka," I said. "That entire crew despises me."

"Why," Isis asked.

"It's because a long time ago, when Jayla use to go to school, we were close. But then one day she became friends with the Hoodys, and our friendship ended."

"You weren't friends just because of that?" Isis asked.

"Well, later on Jayla and the crew started picking on me," I replied. "They even nicknamed themselves 'the Hoodys,'" I said.

"Well, that fits them, the hood rats," Isis said.

"Luckily Jayla left the school, but the Hoodys never stopped bothering me," I said.

"Looks like we will have to fix that," Isis said, looking suspicious.

"Please don't do anything they will blame me for," I said sternly. "I still have another three years of high school with them."

"Which gives us more time to get even," Isis said. I watched her as she struck out of the coat rack we had been hiding behind.

"Isis, come back here," I whispered. But she was already gone. I left the coat rack, hoping that the Hoodys would not see me. I tried to get closer to Isis, but I couldn't without getting caught. I heard Isis whisper something under her breath, but I just couldn't make it out. I saw Isis point her finger at the Hoodys, but I was not about to let the Hoodys see me.

"If you want to be mean and not be nice you shall pay the price. Swoop," I heard Isis quietly say.

I looked up, and all of the hats that were hanging on the shelves came tumbling down. There were so many of all different colors, and every single one came tumbling down right on the Hoodys' heads. As soon as the hats fell on the Hoodys, the shelf dropped. Jayla pushed Kaseena in front of her, and the shelf hit Kaseena's head. Two store employees ran over to help them. The manager ran from the cash register to see what had happened. "What's going on here, girls?" said the manager. The Hoodys were still covered in piles of hats.

I quickly walked out of the store. Isis ran behind me in a big rush. "My mom is waiting for us," she said.

"Oh now you want to leave," I said. "What on earth happened back there?"

"I don't know," she replied. But I knew she knew something; it wasn't common for shelves to fall down on someone, especially in a store. Something about Isis just wasn't right. At that moment, I knew she was a girl that could make things happen without getting caught. I began to reminisce on what had gone on, and I remembered I had heard her say the word "swoop."

By the time I was outside the mall, Isis saw her mom's car. We both ran over and got in. "How was the mall, girls?" Isis's mom asked, trying to make conversion.

"Great!" I said, trying to shut her up.

"Relax," Isis whispered in my ear.

"Okay," I replied in a frustrated tone.

By the time we got home, I didn't really want to talk to Isis. I thought she could give me an explanation as to what had really happened. But little did I know Isis had a way of hiding everything that was the truth. "Do you want to talk about what happened back there"? I asked.

"What?" she said, trying to avoid the subject.

"You know what," I said, wanting to get more out of her. I knew something was up; I just couldn't get her to talk about it.

"So what's a normal school day at school for you?" Isis asked, trying to change the subject.

"Stressful," I replied.

"Oh? What makes it so stressful?" she asked, wanting to get more information out of me.

"Um, there are a lot of bullies and people who just don't like me."

"Why?" Isis asked.

"Well, it's such a long story. It's basically what I told you at the mall, but a little worse," I said, with a little fear in my voice. "Well, enough about me; what's your school like?" I asked.

"Fun," Isis replied in a creepy little voice. "I have teachers eating out of the palms of my hands—and the students."

"Oh Isis, how I wish I had the bravery you have! How do you do it?"

"Let's just say I have a few magic powers up my sleeve," Isis said.

"Very funny. If I could have those powers for one day, I would be so happy," I said with a sad puppy dog face. "I feel I have always lacked some sort of confidence in my life."

Isis looked at me as if I were a patient of hers in a hospital. "I feel so bad for you," she said. "Are you picked on a lot in school?"

I couldn't lie to her; I knew I had to tell the truth. "Yes," I said, hesitating.

"Well, I will just have to fix that," she said in a very rude tone.

"How? You live too far away," I said.

"True," she said. "But throughout life you have to learn to find yourself, and confidence. Not everyone will like you, but you have to be the one to make them respect you." Isis had a spark to her, a wonderful fire that never stopped burning. If someone were to blow that fire out, she would make sure it was reignited. Where could I find that fire?

Isis got up and walked to the mirror in my bedroom, where she looked at herself. She seemed like the kind of girl that idolizes herself a lot.

"So what's a normal school day for you like, Isis?" I asked, hoping she would tell me some of her flaws.

"Honestly? Perfect," she said without a doubting it. "I think my classmates respect me because their intimidated by me," she said.

"Oh, and as for the teachers, they practically eat out of the palm of my hand," she said with a lot of sarcasm in her voice. She winked at me and started to fix her hair in my mirror.

"I really wish I could feel that way about myself," I said, looking down at the floor.

"What's stopping you?" she asked.

"People who really despise me at school," I said, looking at her.

Isis sighed and looked me up and down. "Come here, Tory," she said in a demanding tone. "Look in the mirror; what do you see?"

I didn't really know what to say; I was scared to even say anything. "I see a mirror," I replied.

"Can I tell you what I see?" she said. "I see a girl trapped in a shell that really wants to come out."

Isis was a girl that had a way with people. She could reach out to others and make them believe what she wanted them to believe.

"Isis, are you going to tell me what's going on here?" I asked, wanting a real answer.

"What do you mean?" she said, looking perplexed. I knew I had to tell her, but I didn't know how. I was changing the subject. I couldn't help myself; I was determined to get the answer I wanted.

"Isis, you are going to tell me the truth," I said with anger in my voice.

"I can't," she replied.

"So long for friendship," I said with disappointment. I started to walk toward the door.

"Look, if I tell you the truth, you have to promise not to tell anybody," she whispered.

"Okay, I won't," I replied. "I'm a bird that can fly at night," I said sarcastically.

"You take me as a joke, don't you," she said.

"I do," I said.

Isis pointed her finger straight at me and looked me in the eye. I began to shake as if I were going into shock. "If you want to be mean and not be nice, you shall pay the price. Swoop."

At that moment, everything in the room started to shake, as if an earthquake were taking place. I fell to the ground, shaking in fear, wondering what would happen.

"Wow. Aah!" I screamed.

I heard footsteps running up the stairs to my room.

"Is everything okay girls?" my mom asked with fear in her voice.

"I think we just had an earthquake," Isis said. She acted as if she didn't know what was going on.

"Tory! You all right, honey?" my mom asked with concern. I got up from the floor very slowly, as scared as ever.

"I'm fine, Mom; just slipped," I replied, lying through my teeth.

My mom left the room really believing it was a small earthquake, but I was more freaked out than ever. I knew it wasn't an earthquake; it was a spell. I knew I wasn't crazy either. That was the first time I discovered something not realistic. I believed that we all lived in reality till that day!

Chapter 12

Powers

I looked at Isis with such disbelief; I had a cousin from Jersey that was a witch. This couldn't be true. Or was it true?

"You believe me now?" Isis said, looking at me.

"Do I have any other choice but to?" I replied with sarcasm. There were so many questions running through my mind. I was going crazy within myself. "Isis, how the heck did you do that?" I asked.

"I'm sure you have a lot of questions for me, Tory," Isis replied.

"More than you will ever know, I responded. "Tell me where these powers come from?"

"You can't tell Tory," Isis said. "Not even my parents know about this." She looked very serious.

"I won't; your secrets are safe with me," I promised her. "Just tell me where they come from."

Isis put her hand out in front of me. I looked closely at it, praying that nothing would happen. She slid a blue ring off her finger. I hadn't noticed the ring on her before. "Tory, do you know what this is?" she asked.

I gave her a perplexed look, trying to figure out everything. "Yes, it's a blue ring," I replied.

Isis opened my hand and placed the ring on my palm. I looked closely at it; to me it just looked like an ordinary ring. I then looked at the bottom of the ring. There was engraved the word "Swoop." I knew at that moment why all of those weird things kept happening every time I heard that word. "So this isn't just an ordinary ring, is it?" I asked.

"No," Isis answered. I looked at her with such disbelief. How could a little blue ring have so much power inside it?

"Is this ring making all these strange things happen all day?" I asked.

"Tory, this ring is very special. I found it on a beach when I was only four years old," she said. "I discovered it had powers when I was only ten. I kept it all this time, using magic against those who deserved it."

"Wow!" I said. "I really need that power."

"That's why I am going to give it to you."

"Really?" I said with enthusiasm.

"Yes, Tory. I don't like what you're up against in your school," she said, sympathizing with my emotional pain. "Do something marvelous with it. Just promise me one thing."

"What's that?" I asked.

"Do not take it for granted," she said in a stern tone. "Only use it for little pranks on people who deserve it. Because if you take the ring for granted, it will lose its power."

"Why do you want me to have this? Why are you giving up something so precious?" I asked.

"Because you're my cousin and you need it more than I do to get through your high school journey," she replied.

"Isis, I don't know what to say."

Don't get me wrong; I was really happy when Isis offered me the ring. But I was confused, as it was a very powerful ring, and I could do a lot of things with it. I hadn't known Isis for long enough that I felt comfortable taking items from her. But I really do believe she was right. I had to take this ring through high school to fight back against those who I felt were my enemies. These people at my school stressed me to the point where I was breaking out in hives. These people were coming into my dreams while I was asleep. I knew I had to put an end to this, and this ring would help me do it!

I knew Isis would need to depart eventually, but I also knew that I needed the ring to survive. My high school nightmare wouldn't be over unless I had a little bit of power to accomplish my task. This was my destiny that would finally pave my way into a clearer high school dream. This was definitely the ring for me. It was more than just a piece of jewelry; it was powerful. I needed it for many reasons that I couldn't even think of. I was excited to experience what this ring could do, but I was also a little more anxious for revenge.

It was soon time for Isis to depart. My family was gathered in the living room, saying their good-byes. I knew that it was time to say my good-byes as well. Angel came over and gave me a huge hug that would have made a teddy bear feel loved. Her brother gave me a huge hug as well. I had never felt so happy inside to be with family. When everyone was saying good-bye, Isis gave me a hug. She got really close to my ear so no one could hear her. "Remember what I told you," she whispered. I was very nervous when she said those words. It sent chills up my spine. I kept asking myself whether I was ready for this. I needed a friend, but Isis was gone. Now I had a ring that could be there for me as a friend. Every time I looked at it, it reminded me of Isis. I put the ring on my index finger and wore it proudly. Isis's family was gone, and there I was, standing with the ring. This was a ring that had a lot of power and could make many miracles happen. Here it was on my index finger, I could do anything I wanted with it.

What would you do if you had the most powerful ring in the world?

Chapter 13

Tory's

Break was finally over, and it was time to go back to school and be a part of the horrible chaos of high school. I hated the bad language I encountered along with the intense drama. I walked into the school, and there was no surprise; it looked just like my nightmare from days before. Some things just never change.

I walked in slowly, which was a sad, stressful moment. "You have to come in sometime Tory," said Mrs. Ma-Donny. "I am really glad that I ran into you to talk to you. Tory, honey, if you don't get your grades up, you will be held back."

"What?" I replied in a sad voice.

"Just get those grades up and you won't have to worry," she said with her happy, jolly attitude. This teacher was one of those people whose true intentions you could never really know. She was always a mystery. There were days she was phony and always happy. I knew I couldn't trust her; I just had to deal with her. "I hope you remembered the big test we have in English today on the book *Roots*," she said, giving me a look. I had completely forgotten about the big test on that book about slaves. I had been so busy with Isis over break that it completely left my mind. I knew that I had to pass this test; there was no way I wanted to be kept back to repeat the entire process.

The Hoodys walked by like gods on pedestals. "Hey Tory," the Hulk said as she snickered to Lyka.

"Your hair is ugly," Lyka said in a rude voice. I wanted to say something back, but I just didn't have the strength to. I looked down, and that's when I saw the ring. That's when I finally gained the strength and the power to say what I needed to, or even do what I knew I had to. I looked at the ring much harder than I had before. This time I did it with instant rage. I knew how to use this thing; I just needed confidence. "If you want to be mean and not be nice, you shall pay the price. Swoop," I said in a whisper.

All of a sudden the lunch lady walked by with a disgusting pan of pasta. The students never ate the food; I don't think even a dog would eat it. The pasta from a distance looked as if it was moving; it started to bubble like boiling water. I thought I was seeing things, but the food was weird from a distance anyway. The lunch lady had heels on that day. She walked down the stairs, trying to make her way to the lunchroom. All of a sudden she slipped, and the pasta went flying out of the pan with triple force. I saw Hulk and Lyka walking right by. But before I could say "Watch out," the two girls were already covered in pasta. The Hulk had noodles coming out of her nose. I guess some things don't change; she looked even more like the beast she was before. As for Lyka, who had made that rude remark, her hair was entirely covered in pasta. If my hair was ugly that day, hers was stringy pasta.

I felt so powerful at that moment. This ring was forever my friend. I was shocked when it completely destroyed the two Hoodys. I loved what the ring could do; I even loved the funny writing on the back of it: "Swoop." Lyka and the Hulk were laughed at so hard I don't think I heard them speak for the rest of the day. But I still had a full day ahead of me. The ring gave me a power that I had never had before, which was confidence. I felt as if nothing in the world would or could hurt me as long as I had the ring.

I started to walk to my locker, and Kingston came up from behind me and gave me a huge hug. "Did you see what happened to your enemies?" he asked.

"I did," I said as if I were clueless. I promised myself not to tell anyone what my special ring could do. But I was going to use it if anyone did me wrong. Now I was just waiting to see if anyone else would try to mess up my day. If someone did, I would feel so happy to use my new and improved blue ring.

Before I knew it, the bell rang and it was time for class. It was time for the English course that I had been failing. I knew I was going to fail; I didn't think any ring would help me pass a test. I sat down, trying to breathe. *How will I pass?* I picked up my black pen and looked at the first pages of the test. I had no idea what to do, but I would have to complete the task. Mrs. Ma-Donny kept trying to talk about the test the entire time. She always tried to give us motivational words before a test. I just wanted to tell her shut up and say it wasn't helping.

I didn't know what any of the answers were, but I could see the first set of questions was multiple choice. My first option was to guess and hope I got a good grade. Little did I know I wouldn't have to with my ring on my hand. At that moment, all of a sudden, the pen did the work for me. I started writing extremely fast with my right hand. I could see the ring glowing, and all the answers were coming to me clearly. It was like the ring did the work for me, only I did it myself. By the time the test was over, the ring had made me write so fast that my hand was in pain.

"Pass them up," said Mrs. Ma-Donny. Everyone left the room, drained from the test. I just hoped I had passed the exam. I couldn't afford to fail anything else, or I would have to repeat ninth grade. The ring was extremely powerful; not only could it make my enemies sorry, but it could also make my grades in school much better. I needed this ring more than anything. It couldn't have come into my life at a better time. I was a young girl that needed a source—a way to get revenge against those who did me wrong every school day. I could even be a straight-A student with the magic I had within the ring.

All day I couldn't stop looking at the ring and the way it glowed. I felt that I was in some kind of fantasy. Finding something as powerful as this was nothing but a dream. I had magic in this ring, which was more than amazing. I couldn't wait to tell Isis how my first day with the ring had gone. I wanted to text her a million words about what the ring had done. But I still had a school day to complete. It was a big change in my life to finally have something by my side. This ring was my friend and my way of revenge. After school I lay down on my bed to do homework. I couldn't wait for my phone to ring so I could tell Isis everything that had happened. Then it finally did, when I was least expecting it.

"Hello, Isis," I said with a happy voice.

"Hey, Tory," Isis said. "How has the ring been taking care of you?"

"Really good," I replied with enthusiasm

"Remember not to take advantage of the ring, because it will lose its power," she said in a stern tone.

"I have been gentle and careful," I said with a little voice. "Do you still want the ring back eventually?"

"No, keep it and have it," she said.

"You really want to give up something so powerful?" I asked.

"I'm sure, Tory; It's yours to keep," she said. "Feel free to do whatever you want with it. Well, I have to go, but we will chat soon." She sounded as if she were in a rush.

Isis hung up the phone before I could say much more. I was happy, but at the same time I was scared. I hoped Isis would never hurt me. I loved and honored our friendship, and I didn't want to think she would give me this ring knowing it had bad intentions. I guessed that while I had it I could make other people's lives miserable.

I continued to complete my homework until I heard a knock on my door. "Tory, honey, dinner is ready," my mom said. As I went down the stairs, making my way to the kitchen, I couldn't get the ring out of my mind. The ring was now a big factor in my life; it meant a lot to me. I didn't want to take advantage of its power, but I didn't want to not use it either.

At the dinner table I began to eat slowly; the ring was still on my mind. "How was school?" my dad asked, trying to make conversation.

"Fine," I replied.

When dinner was over, all I wanted to do was get back to playing with the ring. "Tory, after dinner, clean up the kitchen," my mom said in a stern voice.

"I always do that," I said.

"And I always cook," she replied, giving me sass in her voice.

"And I always work," my dad said.

My parents left the room, leaving me with the messiest kitchen to clean. I started to collect the plates off the table. I was about to wash the dishes when I looked down at the ring. I wondered what else it could do. I put my hands on the dishes, with the blue ring shining on top of my fingers. I whispered the word "swoop" under my breath. All of a sudden, before my eyes was an empty sink. Every dish had been washed, and everything in the kitchen was spotless. The power of this ring was unspeakable; it was amazing. There was nothing I couldn't do with this powerful piece of jewelry. It wasn't just something that helped me get revenge; it was something that did my chores for me. I was the most powerful girl in the world. I wanted to do more with this ring and eventually get rid of all of my obstacles.

I went up the stairs and into my bedroom, where I looked at the blue ring. I kept trying to take my mind off it, but it was controlling me. I just had to play with it more and more. I gazed at the ring as it glowed and gleamed with all its power. I couldn't stop staring at it.

Then my room door burst open. "Good job with the kitchen," my mom said. "How did you clean it so fast?"

"Just a swoop of magic I guess," I said with sarcasm in my voice.

"Who gave you that ring?" she asked.

"Just a friend," I said, trying to shut her up.

I ran to the bathroom, trying to avoid her. I didn't want anyone to know about this secret. I didn't even want to tell Kingston. It was just too sacred to show the world. My little powerful secret was forever mine to keep in my heart.

It was time to complete my homework, and I wasn't even tired, because the ring had done all of the work for me. I couldn't stop looking at the round wonderful ring on my finger. It made me so happy to have a friend by my side, but my friend was a ring. I could accomplish anything I wanted to by using this ring. No one knew but me, myself, and I.

I ran upstairs to complete my homework, which was algebra. Math was always a struggle for me, and still is in high school. I lay on my bed and then picked up my pencils to do my math homework. I hated that when it came to a math problem, I would never know if my answer was right or wrong. I solved the first algebraic problem and then began to pout because I didn't know if it was right or wrong. All of a sudden I looked at the oval-shaped blue ring. "Swoop," I said, waiting anxiously for something to happen. I looked at the ring, and numbers appeared on my it. They were the answers to my math problem. I couldn't believe I had actually solved it. I guess I was smarter than I thought I was. I began to become obsessed with my homework; I couldn't stop working. I already had the answer key right on my very finger.

It was a miracle for someone like me, who was failing the ninth grade, to have improved so much on her work. It was because of the ring, of course, but I was retaining a lot of information. I actually became more focused on my work and less focused on the bullies in school. I loved this wonderful feeling inside of me; it was a feeling of relief that I couldn't explain.

When I completed my homework, I decided to get ready for bed. I lay in my bed looking at the bright moon. Then I looked at my ring, and it started to glow. I never truly understood the ring or why it glowed. I guess I still had a lot to learn about it, even if it was fun to play with.

Chapter 14

Revenge

Beep, beep, beep. My alarm clock was going off like crazy. The ring stopped glowing on my finger. I didn't know if that was a bad sign or good sign. I got ready for school, dressing in my same old uniform. It was wrinkled and dirty from me not taking care of it. Then I looked at the ring and said that special word: "Swoop!" My raggedy uniform changed drastically in a matter of seconds. My shirt and pants freshly cleaned. My black shoes were shiny, as if they had been buffed by a blacksmith. My old bun that I wore every day that was so tangled you couldn't even pull a rake through it was now straight. When I looked in the mirror I saw Isis staring back at me. But it wasn't Isis; it was me; I was staring at myself. I pushed my hair back behind my ear. and I saw a pair of pretty earrings hanging there; I had never seen them before. I looked closely at my face, which had makeup on it. I noticed what the ring had done to my hair. It was long, shiny, and straight; it was truly a miracle. This ring had turned me into a supermodel on the go.

"Tory you're going to be late for school," my mother shouted, pushing the door open. "Oh my!"

"What?" I replied.

"Your hair actually looks good," she said with sarcasm in her voice.

I gave her a look of disappointment.

I was happy that she had noticed something about me, but now that my mom was complimenting me, I knew that I had looked horrible all the time before I had the ring.

I didn't want to go to school, but something got me out of bed. It was definitely the ring; I mean, come on, don't tell me that if you had something magical on your finger, you wouldn't use it.

My mom gave me a ride to school, and I was ready for my big day. I hated being at the stupid charter school. People tried to fit in with people they hated. I was the school outcast. Moreover, the teachers were just as fake as the students. As I opened the door to my school, I saw my principal smile at me. I tried to smile back, but I just didn't want to. The only thing that made me happy was the ring. I started to walk down the halls of my school, and Kingston walked by me and touched my shoulder.

"Hello, Tory," said Kingston.

"Hello, Kingston," I replied.

Before I knew it the bell rang, and I knew I had to get to class as fast as possible. As I was running to get to class on time, I looked down at the ring. The ring had turned a dark shade of red; it seemed it was trying to warn me of something. I didn't have time to think why. I ran into my math class a couple of seconds late.

When the ring turned red, I was surprised. I didn't think the ring would do harm to me, but only to the people around me. I sat down in math class, and Mr. Slender was right behind me.

"There are consequences for people who are tardy," Mr. Slender said, sounding cruel.

He was holding a red pen and a brown clipboard, which he used to write me a detention slip.

"Don't be late for class!" he said with a stern tone.

"Sorry, Mr. Slender," I replied in a frightened way.

The class started to giggle at me very quietly. Mr. Slender gave me a dirty look because he was upset. The ring started to shake on my hand, and it was still red. It seemed as if the ring had its own personality, along with its own temper. I looked at Mr. Slender, and he was writing a math assignment on the board. He turned around to face the class. Before he could announce anything else about the lesson, his pants fell off his waist, and he was left standing in front of the classroom in his red underwear with polka dots on them. The entire class gasped with surprise. Now Mr. Slender was the center of attention—and not because he was the teacher, but because he was the outcast of the day!

I felt bad that he went through that embarrassment. But it wasn't as if I made that happen. I never even said the word "swoop." I didn't know the ring could work magic without me.

The class was still in deep laughter. Mr. Slender's face was still red from the embarrassment he had just encountered. As for me, I had actually gotten my revenge on a teacher I had never really liked. Teachers think they can always embarrass students and not get the same karma back. I guess the ring was something that could take care of me. It was such a great friend to have for my own good sake.

After class, I was walking down the hall. Everyone at school noticed there was something different about me. I knew it was my new makeover that the ring had given me that day. I felt like a celebrity getting stared at as I walked past everyone. It was as if I were a supermodel on a runway. I still wanted to keep to myself. I didn't know what else the ring could do, but I knew I wanted to find out.

After seeing my teacher's underpants and looking at my shiny ring, I decided to take a bathroom break. I went into the girls' bathroom. When I came out of the stall, I looked in the mirror while washing my hands. The girl I saw wasn't the old me. It was someone else I was staring at. I no longer had my curly, frizzy hair or my glasses on. It was just a whole new me—a changed me. I still felt like myself, yet I didn't see myself. I looked down at the ring on my finger and thought to myself, *Wow! How powerful, how remarkable.* The ring had accomplished all of my dreams and desires. That just made me wonder what else could I do with the ring.

I walked down the hall knowing that I had all the power in the world. I proudly walked into class ten minutes late. Everyone stared at me, but I didn't care; I was developing a sense of confidence within me. I use to have low self-esteem, but something was different about me now. I didn't have low self-esteem at all, but I had cockiness. Cockiness was something I had never felt in my life before. I don't know if it was because of the ring, but I was changing, and I didn't even know if it was for the better. I felt like at times that I was in a dream that was more like a fantasy. I sat down in class, and I could see the Hulk's shadow behind me. I turned around slowly.

"What you looking at?" said the Hulk in her angry voice.

"Obviously nothing," I said, sassing her right back.

"Who you talking to like that," she replied.

"Who else would I be talking to," I said with attitude.

I couldn't believe what I had just said to her. The Hulk rose up out of her seat and walked over to me slowly. The whole class stared at her and me . She looked me right in the eyes.

"Want to say what you said a little louder?" said the Hulk.

It was just my luck; there was no teacher in the room. It was just me in a class of students. The students couldn't care less if I got beaten up or not. I was tired of being bullied. I was tired of people speaking to me any way they felt they could. I rose out of my seat slowly. Then I looked her in the eye like a furious tiger.

"I said, who else would I be talking to," I said with anger in my voice.

The whole class was staring, waiting to see a huge fight. I didn't care if there was a fight or not. I just needed to put an end to me being bullied. As I looked down at my hand, my ring started to turn red. It was as though the ring were feeling my emotions.

The Hulk was about to try to hit me. For some odd reason, I wasn't afraid at all. I looked down at the Hulk's shoes. "If you want to be mean and not be nice, you shall pay the price," I whispered silently to myself. I realized her shoelaces were being tied together. I knew it was because of the ring, and I didn't say anything about the magic I witnessed. The teacher walked into class just in time to prevent our fight. The Hulk wouldn't dare have the nerve to hit me in front of a teacher; she started to walk away. But before I knew it, she tripped over a chair. She fell facedown on the floor. The whole class laughed really loudly.

The ring had helped me get through that moment. I had needed to give the Hulk a taste of her own medicine. It felt great to finally have something magical to depend on. If anyone went near me, all they would hear was the word "swoop."

Chapter 15

Rock Star=Honors

The ring had definitely changed my life completely. I was thankful for it; it was like a fairy godmother made out of jewelry. There wasn't a day I didn't wear it. I became surprised that no one noticed the ring's magic but me. The ring was something I saw as protection; it was my very special safe piece of jewelry. After standing up to the Hulk, I had had enough of the day. I was a young woman who needed a vacation—a break from this entire school.

At the end of the day, it was time for my death. At least that was what I called it when it came time to get my report card! It was time to face the ultimate task of my high school nightmare. I believe everyone has a fear of their very own high school report card. At this particular high school, we can't hide it from our parents. If we have straight A+ grades, our parents still have to see our progress. If we have straight F grades, our parents have to see it and sign off on those bad grades. As for me, I was kind of in the middle when it came to grades. I wasn't the smartest in the class, and I wasn't the dumbest. I was just a girl who prayed that I could get a C+ and call it a day. It's not that I didn't try in school; it's just that I was a girl who struggled. When I studied all night, I still sometimes got low grades. When I didn't study at all, I would get an F. The huge F on my paper definitely didn't mean "fabulous." It meant "failure" on my work, and good luck getting into college.

I waited patiently in line for my report card. I wasn't anxious, and I wasn't worried. But I most definitely wasn't happy. As I waited in line, I became bored out of my mind. The ghetto girls were standing right in front of me, making a lot of noise. Modeya turned around and then looked at me with and evil glare.

"What are you waiting for?" Modeya asked.

"I am waiting for what everyone else is waiting for," I responded with attitude in my voice.

"Don't get smart, sweetie," said Takeya.

"I am very smart," I replied.

"Someone has developed a tough ego," said Modeya.

"Yes I have!" I replied, feeling a sense of confidence.

"Funny, it's nice that you don't let anyone bully you anymore," said Takeya.

"Why do you feel the need to bully me?" I asked, trying to search for an answer.

"Well everyone in this school is a part of a clique," Takeya replied.

"You're the only outcast and that's why you're bullied!" Modeya said.

"My job was never to fit in here; it was just to get an education," I said with attitude.

The ghetto girls walked away and looked at their report cards elsewhere.

I didn't want to pick up my report card, but I also didn't want to leave it there. If I left it, they would mail it to my house, so I was backed into a corner no matter what. As the line started to move forward, I became more nervous. I took my report card and ran into the bathroom. I locked myself in the bathroom stall. I started to cry my eyes out before I even opened my report card. I knew that my grades would be failing. It was because of Mrs. Ma-Donny always smiling at me, and then giving me bad grades on my essays at the end of the day. I didn't want to open it, but I knew that I had to. I slowly opened the little brown paper package it came in. It was smooth and as light as a feather. As I slowly opened it, I could feel the tears run slowly down my face. I wiped them away and opened the package even more slowly.

As I looked down at my hand, I saw that the ring was turning yellow. The ring was as yellow as the sun. It began to shine brightly. I looked down at my report card and saw that "A+" happened to appear all the way down the paper. I couldn't believe my eyes; this was something that had never happened to me before. Maybe I was a genius, maybe I was lucky, or maybe I was just fortunate to have a magical ring on my finger.

Not only did I feel powerful; I also felt like a rock star at the same time. I had never gotten good grades before. I had always been a C+ student. The ring was really changing my life and my grades.

I was learning more and more about the ring as time went on. I started to map out in my mind what happened to the ring each time it glowed. The original color was blue, and when it fought my battles, it was red. When I cried and it came time to make my day shine, the ring would turn a shade of yellow as bright as the sun. The sun was one of the things that made me happy in life.

One thing I admired about the ring was that it gave me something I had never had within myself; I gained faith within me. I was so thankful for the ring, because it gave me an unthinkable strength that I never thought I had.

After a wonderful report card day, I couldn't wait to go home and show my mom. When I looked at the report card, I began to remember the times in my past life when I came home with many bad grades on my report card. My mother would just yell at me at the top of her lungs, thinking those bad grades should change. I knew the grades needed to change; the problem was that I struggled in school. I really didn't know how to change them at all.

Even though I was happy about the report card, I knew the ring had changed the real grades. I knew what the ring had done was wrong. I couldn't depend on a ring changing everything for me in life. I knew that I would eventually have to depend on myself and not jewelry. As much as I hated to admit the truth, I knew it was the ring that had taken all the tests for me. Every time I panicked, the ring would shine yellow and do whatever it could. The ring would shine brightly to make me happy again.

The last time I was taking a test in math, a couple of weeks ago, I started to panic, and I let my anxiety take over. Before I knew it I had forgotten all of the answers. The ring made my hand very numb and sore, and took over my entire right hand. It made my hand write all of the correct answers. It even solved all of the math equations I needed to know. The ring was a genius within itself. I just wished I were the genius and not a piece of jewelry.

I took the bus home and wanted to just really think by myself. Kingston sat right beside me on the bus, but I was so wrapped up in my thoughts I didn't even know he was there.

"Hello, Tory," he said, trying to get my attention.

"Hey, Kingston, I didn't even realize you were there."

"You seem frustrated and deep in thought," he said in a concerned tone.

"I am; you have no idea," I said softly with a sigh in my voice.

"How has everything been?" he asked.

"Good," I replied.

"Did you get your report card?"

"I did," I replied.

We both looked at each other on the bus and switched report cards. I looked at his, and he looked at mine. When I saw Kingston's report card, I felt as if I were looking at mine, because I was used to getting bad grades. Every bad grade you could think of was on his card. He even got an I, which meant "incomplete." The thing is, he and I were both used to seeing horrible grades on our report cards. But when he saw mine, everything immediately changed.

"Wow! How did you pull this off, Tory?" he asked in a surprise voice.

"Let's just say I had a little bit of help from a family friend," I said softly.

"Who? And can they tutor me, please?" he asked.

"It depends on if you wear jewelry," I mumbled under my breath.

"What?" Kingston asked.

"Nothing," I quickly replied.

"I am glad I ran into you, because there is something I have to tell you," Kingston said in a very sad voice.

My heart started to beat as fast as it could. I had no idea what he wanted to tell me, but judging by his tone, it wasn't too good.

"What is it?" I asked

"I'm going to a new school," Kingston said.

"Why?" I asked.

"I have been getting such bad grades that my parents want to take me out of Haltom High school," he said.

"I can't go on and continue failing; this charter school is too much for me," he said.

"You can't just leave me here in this school," I said.

"You will be fine. It seems like for the past couple of days things have finally been working out in your favor. You have been getting good grades; people even seem to pick on you less. You don't even need me."

"When do you leave?" I asked.

"I leave in three days," he said.

"What school are you going to?" I asked.

"A boarding school south of New Hampshire; they have tutors and teachers that will give me better academic support," he said.

I wanted to tell Kingston everything that was going on. I wanted to tell him about the ring. I wanted to tell him how I got the grades, and I even wanted to tell him why there was less bulling going on at the school. But I just couldn't tell him everything I wanted to, because Isis had told me not to. First I had lost Lennie, who moved to Florida. Now I was losing Kingston, who was going far away as well. I felt alone, and now that I would have no friends close to me at the school, where would I turn? I would be by myself now that he was leaving. I had been left out by every clique in the school. I had even been left out by those who really feared me. People were now scared to say things to me at the school because they were afraid of what might happen to them. I'm sure people were starting to notice the patterns of incidents related to me. If they were mean to me, something bad would happen to them. People had started to back down; even Kingston had noticed it. But he never knew why at all. I couldn't picture high school without my best friend. It was just something I would have to get over and get used to you.

As I was walking home, I was happy but sad. I had a great report card to show my parents, but my best friend was leaving in three days. I didn't really want to speak to anybody. I had thought the enemies of high school were my only battle. But I guess in life you learn there are a lot of things to think about other than just getting back at your enemies. There are just things that are far more important. I said "swoop" one hundred times to change Kingston's mind about leaving the school. Unfortunately, the ring couldn't make Kingston change his mind. The ring couldn't stop a person's free will. All the ring did was turn pitch black. I guess it didn't have all of the powers that I wanted it to have. It just had simple magic.

I was blessed to have it but was sad to lose my friend.

Chapter 16

Orange

When I got off the bus, I ran to my room and locked the door. I was so upset about the news I had been given. The ring couldn't make my best friend stay; nor could it bring him back to me. I wished I could just change everything that had happened. I threw myself on the bed, crying silently to myself. I then heard a voice outside my bedroom door.

"Tory, come out of that room right now," my mother said.

"I'm busy," I said angrily.

"Watch the tone, Tory," my mother said softly. "I know you're upset because of your report card, but I'm going to have to see it sometime soon."

My mom came right into the room, picked up my backpack, and shook it really hard.

"What are the grades?" she asked.

The report card fell onto the floor beside my mother's foot. She slowly picked it up and opened it. I don't think I have ever seen her face look so surprised. She looked at every single subject on the report card.

"Oh my, Tory!" she said enthusiastically. "I can't believe this."

"Neither can I," I said, trying to stay calm.

Little did my mom know that that my grades weren't the reason I was crying. I was losing my best friend, and the ring couldn't change it. I wanted to tell my mom about Kingston, but I also wanted to keep my misery to myself. I was very unhappy because of the absence of Kingston that would soon occur.

"No wonder you're crying," she said. "You have never had a report card this good. I can't wait to show your father."

She held it close to her heart and ran out the room with it. Parents usually don't ask much from children other than that they do well in school. The report card reminded me of the times I struggled through school. I was waiting for my mom to yell at me, but the grades were good enough she didn't need to.

I threw myself on the bed, crying my eyes out. I used my hand to wipe away my tears. The ring turned dark brown, but it had been black for the longest time. I was confused about the ring and what was happening. I added brown to the record in my head of all the colors the ring had changed to.

Blue = Original Color

Red = Revenge

Yellow = Happiness

Black = Free Will

Brown = Sadness

I was really upset with Isis; she had explained the bare minimum about the ring. She never told me all there was to know about it. I felt I was on my own to learn about the ring. I prayed this wasn't a setup. Let's be honest; I didn't know Isis that well at all. I was just way too vulnerable and trusting.

I finally stopped crying and wiped away my tears. I could feel the last tear roll down my face. The teardrop fell on my ring accidentally. I stared at the ring as it turned oily and then a little watery. I thought it was just because my eyes were wet at first, but that wasn't the case at all; the ring was watery. It started to slowly bubble up right before my eyes. The ring turned a bright shiny shade of orange. I looked closer at the ring; it wasn't my imagination at all. This was really happening. I had learned what all of the other colors meant, but I didn't know what orange meant at all. I prayed that it was something good. I just couldn't handle any more bad news.

As I stared at the ring, I was in such disbelief. I looked closer, and I saw black letters. In my days of using the ring, this had never happened before. The writing on the ring stated, "First make one big wish." I did what the ring told me to do; I made sure it was what I really wanted. I whispered to myself in a quiet voice, "I truly wish I could have my high school life the way I want it!"

I was scared—really upset and afraid. So many emotions ran through my body in so many ways. I was so worried about what would happen next. I was sick of the people in school, sick of the ring, sick of friends, and even sick of grades. I felt there was no escape. Even with the ring I felt alone at times in many ways. I didn't know what the ring was asking me to do, but I did exactly what it told me to do. I looked down at the ring, and it turned a brighter shade of orange. *What could this mean?* I thought. I didn't know, but I wanted it to mean something special. I already was having a bad day, because I felt betrayed by Isis. This cousin of mine had never told me about the things the ring could do. As for school, how was I going to survive without my best friend? I was deep in thought when the ring started to glow. It lit up very bright and shone like a star in the sky. My poor skinny hands started to slowly shake. More letters appeared on the ring, but this time it was sentences: "Now you have made your one big wish. This wish shall now be received and never returned. Now that the wish is complete, there is no way to defeat."

When the ring was finished telling me its little speech, I thought nothing of it. I just wanted to go into a deep sleep. I wanted to forget everything that had happened that day. I needed time to myself, and the only way I could get that was to fall into a long, dark sleep. At that moment, I fell asleep in my uniform; I didn't even care. Before I knew it, the moon was slowly coming up, and the sun slowly vanished. I was so depressed that I didn't even eat dinner. I was sound asleep with no disturbance in the world.

Chapter 17

A Student and a Princess

As I rolled over in my bed and tossed and turned in my sleep, I could feel my body become a little bit weak. I opened my eyes very slowly, and all I saw was a huge ray of sun in my eyes. Kingston was forever out of the picture, and my life would go back to the way it was: no friends, no one in my life, and no nothing, I guess.

I walked to the bathroom to get myself ready for school. Believe it or not, I was still half asleep. I couldn't tell you what was going on around me at all. I think a part of me was sleepwalking. As I looked at the mirror above the bathroom sink, I stared very hard at myself and studied myself in the mirror. As I went for my toothbrush on the side of the sink, I saw the ring on my finger glowing bright orange. What scared me about this was that the ring hadn't yet gone back to its original color. It was now orange and very bright; there was not a single shade of blue on it.

I walked out of my bathroom looking confused. I didn't know if orange meant something bad. But what I did know was that I had made a big wish the night before. I had been so angry then that I couldn't even remember what my wish was about.

I walked straight into my bedroom, by now more awake. As I opened my bedroom door, I saw a completely different room than the one I had been in the night before. I had been so busy sleepwalking I hadn't even noticed my room had changed. The entire room was different;

it had been transformed. My bed was a little smaller; it had changed from a full-size bed to a twin bed. My walls were painted a light shade of purple and had posters all over them. Last time I checked, my walls were pink, not purple. On the left side of my bed was a huge window through which I could watch the sun set.

I was staring all around my room. I had posters of all my favorite sports that I wanted to play in high school but I never hid because I was afraid people would make fun of me. Next to the super big window was a huge pair of red and white pom-poms. They looked huge even from the distance I was standing from them. I looked at the closet and saw a red-and-white cheerleading uniform with my high school's name on it. I didn't think it was really mine, but I guess it was, as it was in my room. I looked where my desk normally was and saw a small white wooden desk. The desk held my computer nice and high.

I looked on the wall beside the desk and saw pictures of me with people from my high school. Some of them were people I would never speak to in a million years. I had pictures of me and the Hulk smiling together, holding up gold medals. We were both dressed in swim team bathing suits, standing near a pool. I knew my school had a pool, but I never went there. I had always wanted to join the swim team but never thought I was never good enough. I never really gave myself a chance. So when I saw a picture of myself near the pool, especially standing beside the Hulk, I was speechless for very long time. It made me want to study the pictures more closely. I didn't quite get why this was happening or why the entire universe had turned completely upside down. But one thing I knew was that my life was a new life.

I stared harder at the pictures, and above the pictures were more pictures of me in a cheerleading uniform. I must say I looked really good in that uniform. I was a good-looking individual, and my hair was so pretty! I didn't even look like the real me. I always wore my hair in a bun, because I was afraid of what the girls would do to it in school. When I looked at the picture more closely, I looked at other girls surrounding me as well. In one, I was at the top of a pyramid with all the other girls below me. Members of the Exclusive Clique were holding me up, and the Quiet Girls were standing beside them. I had a huge banner on the wall as well that read, "Head Cheerleader!" I looked at all of the pictures in such a confused way. I would never have gone out for the cheerleading team. I never thought I was good enough or that type of girl. I knew that almost everybody was involved in some clique or sport in school, but I never had the desire to be in one, because I was just too shy and afraid.

I stepped back from the pictures very slowly and tried to think about what was going on. As I moved back, I slipped on a ball. I was really scared of what I tripped over. A volleyball slowly rolled behind me. I asked myself, *Where did that come from?* I picked it up. I then looked up to see a huge poster of me on the wall, holding the volleyball. I was posing like a model or a volleyball pro. I couldn't believe my eyes, and I was so frustrated, because I didn't realize what was going on at first.

I walked over to my computer and opened it up. On the screen I saw my high school newspaper. The bottom of the paper had my name on it. Not only was it highlighted in black, but it also stated "Editor-in-Chief Victoria Morton." I was shocked. I was actually the editor-in-chief of the newspaper. I was the head cheerleader, a swimmer, and a volleyball player. This was definitely a dream that I was supposed to wake up from. I didn't know the ring could make all this happen in just one night. This was extraordinarily remarkable.

I heard a knock at the door. I was scared to see what was behind it.

"Who is it?" I said.

My mother burst into my room. "Come on, you are going to be late for school," she said.

"Mom, don't you notice something different about my room?" I asked.

"Yes, dear, it's clean for once," she said, not looking surprised.

"It was a good idea for you and your friends to come over and decorate," she said.

"I remember none of this," I said, looking surprised.

"We don't have time this morning. Put on your cheerleading uniform," she said, sounding as if she were in a hurry.

I got dressed in my room, but I still had no idea what was going on. I quickly put on my uniform and ran downstairs.

"You missed your bus, honey; I will drive you to school," my dad said.

I ran to the car with my backpack and computer. My parents seemed the same, but everything had changed before my eyes. I was very confused at first, but I can't say that I didn't like my new room. The rest of the house was the same.

On the ride to school, I stared closely at the ring. It was so orange and bright that I started to wonder what it might make happen. When my dad pulled up to the school, I was there in time. I started to exit the car, but my dad stopped me. "By the way honey, congratulations!" he said with a smile on his face.

I didn't know what my dad was talking about, but I had a feeling I would soon find out.

I walked right into my school, feeling a sense of pain in my stomach. The pain was from anxiety because I didn't know what the ring had done. What if I walked into school clueless about my entire life?

As I took my first steps into my school there were people smiling at me from a mile away. I didn't know what they were smiling at, but I looked behind me because I was for sure it wasn't me. As I got into the hallway there were people coming from behind me.

"Congratulations, Tory," a girl said.

"Well done, Tory," a boy said.

I didn't know what was going on, but I was about to find out. I was happy and content though, because I had been in school for three minutes and no one had said anything cruel. I walked toward my locker, and on the wall near my locker was a huge sign. The sign stated, "Editor-in-Chief." I was so happy to see that sign, but I was also shocked. I knew I was a great writer, but I had never tried try to become the editor-in-chief. I didn't think anyone would vote for me, much less nominate me. I never gave anything in high school my best shot.

I went to open my locker that I had forgotten to lock. I recalled that the last time I forgot to lock my locker, I ended up with tons of eggs in there. The Hoodys always played horrible pranks. I to opened the locker very slowly, but instead of eggs, there were balloons as big as my locker, and the balloons read, "Congrats, Editor!" I wondered who these could be from; I was so shocked and amazed. I knew they weren't from Kingston, because he had left the school. I didn't have any other friends in the school, so I was really shocked!

"Do you like the balloons?" I heard from behind me.

"Who said that?" I asked, looking perplexed.

"Over here, Tory," Kadence said.

I couldn't believe she was speaking to me. The only person Kadence ever spoke to in high school was her man. Lawrence walked right up to my locker, and so did Patience and Joey.

"We all wanted to surprise you," said Lawrence.

"We put the balloons in your locker because we knew that you would be elected editor-in-chief," said Joey.

"I am sorry not to be the bearer of bad news, but I didn't know we spoke," I said looking confused.

"Well, we have been speaking for weeks, ever since you started the Newspaper Club," said Patience.

"Kadence and Patience write poetry, and Lawrence and I write news," said Joey.

"As for you, you're the editor-in-chief of the newspaper," said Kadence.

"Did you, like, hit your head or something?" asked Lawrence.

"No, just woke up in a new universe," I said in a soft voice.

The bell rang. I grabbed my books and ran to my next class. When I walked into Ms. Jackolantern's class, everyone was already seated. I quickly sat down before she thought I was late. As she walked into the room, looking professional, she stared at me very hard, but in a kind manner.

"Please stand, Tory," she said in a demanding tone. "This is your new editor-in-chief!" she shouted out to the class.

The entire class clapped for me, and I almost cried my eyes out. I had never felt so special, and I had never gotten so much respect in my school. I felt as if this were all a dream, but it was my own reality.

"Congrats, Tory!" Ms. Jackolantern said in a proud voice. "Please feel free to make your speech about the way you are feeling. And tell us what you want to bring to our school using the newspaper."

I hated making speeches. The last time I made one, I got made fun of. I walked up to the front of the class, my heart beating as fast as a horse can run. My legs were shaking as if I were on some kind of medication. But my ring was glowing, so I felt safe.

"I am so honored to be the editor-in-chief of our newspaper. I want us to come together as one and add more and more ideas to our school as we begin to grow. Let us not forget the members that have helped us develop the news every day: our students, our teachers, and, last but not least, our school board. As we begin to create a wonderful school, let our newspaper highlight the main topics of what we have achieved." I said these powerful words strongly and with a great deal of power in my voice.

The AC in the classroom blew my hair softly, but this time I didn't feel cold; I felt like a model with the wind blowing in my hair. My cheerleading uniform began to blow blissfully as well. The entire class stood up and clapped; my speech was outright phenomenal!

"Congratulations again, Tory," said Ms. Jackolantern.

"She is captain of the cheerleading team, captain of the volleyball team, captain of the swim team, and now editor-in-chief of our newspaper," Glow shouted out.

"I have to give it to you, Tory, you're a girl that just may get into Harvard," said the Hulk.

I couldn't believe what my school had turned into. It was as if the ring had given me the impossible. I mean, I wasn't complaining; I was so excited to see what the rest of the day would be like!

Before I knew it, it was time for gym class. I was so scared to go to gym after my horrible nightmares of people chasing me out of class, and also because of the way the cliques in my school treated me. But with the ring I had nothing to worry about. I knew the ring would take very good care of me.

As I walked to my gym class, I reminisced on my two favorite friends that were no longer at my high school; Lenny and Kingston, whom I missed so dearly, were gone forever. I could never share these wonderful memories with them. It was as if I had become a whole new person after they left. The thought of my two very good friends not being part of my high school life brought tears to my eyes. When I looked down at the ring, it turned brown. I guess it could sense that I was a sad individual.

As I walked farther down the hall, I noticed a huge sign on the wall. The sign stated in big letters, "SCHOOL DANCE THIS SATURDAY! THE FRESHMAN FORMAL!" I did want to go, but I would have to go alone.

As soon as I lost myself in deep thought, the unthinkable happened before my eyes. All I could hear was the sound of a stampede behind me. It was just like my nightmare, only this time it was really happening. I remembered from my nightmare a stampede of people following me. It was as though my dream came to reality at once, but this time this madness wasn't going away. I tried to run just like I had done in the dream, but I couldn't outrun the stampede of people coming from behind me. I didn't want to have an anxiety attack, but part of me did want to find out what was behind me.

Before I knew it, the stampede had caught up with me. I guess I wasn't that fast of a runner after all. When I looked behind me, every boy clique in the school was surrounding me. I just wanted to go to gym class, but the ring made it a class that it wasn't supposed to be. G-Crew was surrounding me, trying to ask me questions. When I looked over the shoulder of a G-Crew boy, I saw another clique trying to get to me. It was the Trolls, who were trying who grab my hand. I was so scared; I knew that I couldn't get out of this. It was just like the dream I had of everyone in the school chasing me. Every boy clique in the class was trying to ask me out.

"Tory will you go out with me?" Koury asked.

"Tory, will you go with me to the dance?" Mars asked.

"Tory, can you please be my date for the dance," Teddy asked.

Never had I thought all of the boys in the school would go out of their way to ask me out. I was so happy about what was going on, yet I was confused. I felt like a princess who was waiting to choose her prince. There was no way I was going to let this go to my head. It was because of the ring's magic, not the minds of the boys. "It's just the ring's magic," I said to myself. I walked into gym class with a group of boys behind me.

"Well look who's here," said Rashly.

"All of the boys in the school want to date her," shouted Takeya.

I was used to having negative things shouted out to me. But never in a million years did I think this would happen. I was the queen bee—unstoppable. I was in love with myself, but more so in love with the life I had. I was living the new, improved life of a total princess. I felt like a star that everyone wanted to know. The ring made me feel like a total diva. I felt so famous.

I used to feel famous in a bad way in my high school. If my school had ever had a tabloid, I would have been the bad girl who ended up on the cover as a losers for all to make fun of. But, the ring gave me the power of confidence in this school. I went from a weird geek to a princess who was chic. Everyone wanted to be just like me. I was a powerful force, and I loved every bit of it.

As I walked through gym class, the AC that use to freeze me like an ice cube blew my hair with its soft, gentle breeze, and I had a big smile on my face. All of the boys in the class stared at me as if I were a princess waiting to pick her prince. I wished Kenny and Kingston could see what was happening at the school. But they were gone for good, and I was the ruler of this kingdom. The ring was shining bright yellow, and a little orange. My biggest wish had come true, and I was really happy.

By the time the boys stopped staring at me, there was a huge interruption. Mr. Toughneck blew his whistle really loudly. It was time for gym class to start.

"It is now time for a full two hours of gym," Mr. Toughneck announced.

The class sighed.

"Cheerleaders, you may proceed to the right side of the gym and practice your cheers for the rally," Toughneck said in a demanding tone.

All of the cheerleaders started to move to the other side of the gym. I stayed put, not moving a muscle. The Exclusive Clique stared at me hard, along with the rest of the squad.

"Tory, you're the lead; you have to go to the right side of the gym," Toughneck said.

"Oh, I knew that"! I said, acting as if I knew what I was talking about.

The entire cheerleading team waited for me to take my place. I was nervous, and I didn't know what to do. I walked over slowly and hesitantly and approached the other girls. I hoped the ring would help me in cheer practice, because I didn't know anything about cheerleading. The ring turned a little yellow, and I just put all my energy into my voice.

"Gimme an H!" I said really loudly.

"H!" the cheerleaders yelled behind me.

All of the cheerleaders kept yelling the same letters and words I yelled. I continued the cheer as if I knew what I was taking about.

I am not going to lie; I had a lot of fun being the leader. For once in my life I was the one everyone looked at. I wasn't just a person in the crowd. I didn't feel like another number; I was the leader in charge. The ring made this all possible. I was somebody rather than nobody. After an hour of cheer practice had gone by, we still had another hour of gym left. Two hours of gym was like a never ending process. I could hear Mr. Toughneck's whistle blowing loudly across the gym.

"It's time for dodgeball!" Toughneck said extremely loudly.

The boys were walking from the other side of the gym. They had just come from basketball practice.

"Hey, Tory, have you decided who you will be taking to the dance?" asked Koury.

"No, I haven't yet; let me sleep on it," I said quietly.

"The two captains for dodgeball are Kaseena and Koury," Toughneck said loudly.

I was so shocked that we were going to play dodgeball for the last hour of gym. I didn't want balls to be thrown at me at all. I remembered that in middle school I was always picked last to be on a team, because I wasn't that great at sports. The Hulk and the leader of G-Crew were the two captains for dodgeball. I knew that I would be picked last, and that was just sad.

"I pick Tory," Koury said.

"You knew I was going to pick Tory," the Hulk said.

She gave Koury a dirty look and started picking the Exclusive Clique for her team. I was shocked that I was first picked. No one had ever liked me at this school. I was surprised by how quickly people wanted to be my friend and have me on their team.

When the teams were made, everyone went to do team huddles. There were so many cliques against each other. Koury was acting like a king as captain, but he was acting like a mean king.

"Okay, everyone hit everyone with the ball, but make sure we hit Kaseena."

"Why?" I asked Koury.

"Because we don't get along, and it's a game," he said.

"Is that really the right way to do things?" I asked Koury.

"It's the way we do things at Haltom High; we get even with the people we don't like," said Koury.

"Koury, you are crazy," I said.

Mr. Toughneck blew the whistle, and the game began. When balls started flying at me, I just looked at the ring for mercy. By the time I looked up, the people on my team were throwing balls at the Hulk. There were so many balls being thrown in her direction. I can't say I wasn't happy; she had given me a hard time at this school. But I can say I felt bad and sorry for her. Even the Exclusive Clique members were getting tons of balls thrown at them. I loved the sight of payback and revenge, but I remembered the time I was bullied. I remembered the time I was left out, and the times when I felt I had no one. It was my responsibility to use the powers I had to help them, even though these girls had been so mean to me in the past. I wasn't going to let them get bullied, because it was wrong.

"If you want to be mean and not be nice, you shall pay the price. Swoop," I said with rage.

As soon as I said the magic words, the balls that were being thrown at the Hulk went in a completely different direction. The Hulk started to run out of the gym, but all of a sudden she tripped over a red ball that was rolling across the gym floor. The Hulk fell, breaking her right ankle, and she screamed for help. She was in so much pain. Mr. Toughneck blew the whistle, and the entire gym went quiet. In seconds everyone was frozen. Some people were laughing loudly at her being hurt. I can't say I was glad she was hurt; I really felt bad and wanted to help, but she was hurt so badly Mr. Toughneck had to call an ambulance.

"Help, help," the Hulk screamed.

There was nothing I could do but stand there and feel sorry. I didn't know what the ring had done; it seemed to have backfired. I was only trying to help. I didn't mean to hurt her, but I guess I did.

I didn't speak the entire day. The ring was brown all day because I was just so sad. I had sympathy for people; I wasn't one to stand there and laugh. I knew the Hulk had done mean things to me in the past, but I would never want the ring to do something terrible like that. I was really just trying to help, but instead I made everything worse.

Was the ring becoming dangerous?

The gossip about the Hulk filled the school all day. I was silent the entire day, because I didn't know what else to do. I was scared of the ring's power; I hoped I hadn't caused the Hulk's injury. That day, I went from being a princess to feeling like a guilty princess. I ran over the story in my mind. I didn't want to say the ring was the cause, mainly because the ring had given me everything I wanted. It had given me a completely new high school life, a lot of achievements, and good grades I had never thought I could make.

During the course of the day, I couldn't even look at the ring. I feared its power, along with its dangerous intentions. I replayed the story of the Hulk's broken ankle over and over in my head, but it just made me feel a lot worse. I had used the ring to stop terrible things from happening to the Hulk, but she got really hurt in the process, which saddened me so much more. I have a conscience more than anything. I have such a strong conscience that I punish myself before consequences are given.

I walked slowly to my locker, losing myself in thought about the ring. On my locker there was a huge poster, though it looked like a bumper sticker on my locker. "MODELING AUDITIONS HOSTED BY SENIORS TOMMORROW!" I thought about doing some modeling on the side. It would be a fun thing to do for a while. When I was a little girl, I always dreamed about being the next big supermodel, but I never thought I was pretty enough. I thought it would be fun to try it out just one time. I had two more classes before the day was over. I had an English class and an advanced physics class. When Star came up behind me and started to follow me to class, I was a little paranoid because of what had happened to the Hulk. I didn't trust anybody, not one person. I couldn't even trust the ring, because I was so scared. The hallways were starting to get a little crowded as I made my way to English class.

"Have you decided who you want to take to the dance, Tory?" Star asked very loudly.

"Yes, I think I have," I said loudly.

"Who!" Shouted G-Crew and the Peanut Heads.

"Don't tell me you're taking Kingston," said Star.

"Very funny. He is at a boarding school," I said.

"Oh, I didn't even notice he was gone," said Glow.

"No, you wouldn't, would you," I said.

"No, I wouldn't," said Glow.

"Well, girl, you need to pick the boy you're going with," said Modeya in a sassy tone.

"Yeah, because all the boys want you and nobody else until you pick," said Via, sounding really aggravated.

I really couldn't decide. I wished Kingston were there to help me. He had always helped me through everything. Even though I had to make a decision soon, I just thought about the good times we had on my birthday, and even on the day we supported each other when Lennie was leaving. It would be nice to share the ring's power with him. But then the ring would probably lose its power.

"Hello, who are you going to pick?" Via said, interrupting my seven minutes of heaven.

"The guy I choose is Shawn," I said with a sad voice. "I am sorry, G-Crew; I don't want to hurt either one of you!"

"You can't go to the dance with the entire basketball team either," said Modeya.

Everyone was shocked by the news. I guess they had thought it would be Trance or Koury, but I never really liked them like that. I didn't care who they thought they were; my heart had never settled with them. I just picked so the entire school could get off my back and the other girls could have dates for the freshman formal. I was glad it was over with, because the last thing I wanted to do was have a stampede of boys following me, like what happened in my dream not so long ago. I mean, I'd always had a little crush on Shawn. I loved his hazel eyes and his muscular body. I guessed I would see where this might take us.

"So Tory, you picked me today," said Shawn.

"I guess," I said with a hesitant voice.

"I will pick you up at seven at your house on Saturday night," he said.

"I guess I will be there," I said.

The bell rang, and everyone hurried to class. I knew I should be excited about my high school crush asking me out, but I wasn't; I was just feeling a little lost. I don't know exactly why, though. I thought the ring was supposed to solve my problems, But it could change only a few things in my life. It couldn't change my emotion or make me feel I was in the right place. I guess I should be thankful the ring changed my life. But something was really missing, and I couldn't figure out what it was. I was a princess that had lost her crown. I looked down at the ring, and it was very brown. I was glad the ring could see that I was very sad.

Chapter 18

The School Dance

The ring remained a dark shade of brown, but I just ignored it. I didn't want to be reminded that I was sad. I just wanted to be happy for once, because of what the ring had done for me. I mean, everyone in high school wanted to be my friend. My crush from the beginning of freshman year had asked me out. What more could a freshman in high school ask for? I was even getting straight As in school. I mean, this ring didn't work only magic; it worked miracles.

I was thankful and happy, but the ring couldn't bring my best friends back. It couldn't make these people in school genuine or kind. The ring could do only certain magical things, but not all. At this moment all I was thinking about was going to the school dance. I also had to find a way to pay for the dress I wanted. Everyone was going to be dressed up for the formal. I knew I had to find a way to buy a dress. It had to be under $200, and it needed to be a really pretty color that looked good with my skin tone. I had never really cared about my appearance before, but I needed to look good. Everything had changed. I was going with the boy that I had always liked. I needed a dress that spoke out about the way I felt about him.

Unfortunately, all I could think about was Kingston. There, I said it; I wasn't going with the guy I really wanted to go with. I was going with my crush, the guy I barely knew, never really spoke to, and didn't know anything about. What could I do? Kingston wasn't there at all. I knew that I had to find a way to forget about him, or I would never be able to enjoy myself.

The formal was four days away, and I didn't want to ruin it for myself. It was the event that every freshman in school wanted to attend. It was the event where freshmen dressed up their best. The freshman formal was almost like a senior prom. And from what the upperclassmen stated about the freshman formal, every one of the freshman always had a good time there. It was like a huge highlight for the freshman class! I just wanted it to be a highlight for me, even without Kingston there. But it wouldn't be a good time without Kingston at all.

It was so agitating the way I debated with myself over what I was going through. I needed a way to let go of the fact that Kingston was gone forever. As I walked to my study hall session, I realized that my life was really good with the ring, but I was lost without my best friend. I started to lose myself in the process of wondering what could have been between us. As I slowly stepped into study hall, a senior came up behind me.

"Tory, did you sign up for the modeling auditions?" asked the senior.

"No I didn't," I answered, sounding disappointed.

"Well you should," the senior said.

"I will see. I just have a lot on my mind," I said.

"It would be great to have you model; you are the head cheerleader," the senior said. "You are also the most popular freshman in school."

"Thanks!" I said.

I had a lot on my plate with everything that was going on. I didn't really have time for a show. All I had time for was just getting through the year with no drama, and learning how to control the ring. The ring was a powerful force; I grew to know it and love it.

I still wanted to find a way to make my freshman year end well. It had started out in misery, though I never knew why. But because of the ring, I was a person who had complete control of my life. The ring wasn't only my perfect piece of jewelry; it was my best friend—the friend I had wanted in my high school life forever—but only when it made good things happen for me. I can't say I liked all of the bad.

Before I knew it, I had drifted off into my dream world—a world that was just a little easier than the one that I was living in. I walked down the hall, where I saw a line to sign up for the modeling auditions. By the time I got to the front of the line, I saw that there were magazines on the table near the sign-up sheet.

"What is all this"? I asked, looking very perplexed.

"It is the front cover of the high school modeling magazine," said a senior. "It is what the senior modeling club started this year."

"This is so nice!" I said, sounding enthusiastic.

"If you win the modeling show, you get to be on the front of the cover for the entire year," said the senior, "along with a seven-hundred-dollar stipend."

I quickly picked up the pen and signed my name. I knew it would be worth it in the end. I was so happy to finally be a part of this modeling show. First I would have to find a way to at least audition to be in it. I just looked at the ring and thought to myself, *I hope the ring will give me the confidence.*

On my way home, the ring was the furthest thing from my mind, and the modeling show wasn't really that relevant at the moment. All that was relevant was what I would be wearing for the dance and how I would get the money to buy it. I got home and dropped my bag near the door. I ran upstairs to look at my decorative closet and found stuff I never knew I had. My closet was so different and more spacious than my old closet. I looked at the ring, and it glowed its original blue color. I secretly thanked it in my mind. I saw all these pretty dresses I never knew I had. That is, I knew I had them, but I didn't think I would ever wear them. I believed dresses were for girls that were girly, not sporty like I was. I felt sporty every day, not like a girly individual. I guessed I wouldn't have to go to the store after all.

I heard a knock at the door. At first I was scared out of my mind. I had no idea anybody was home.

"Who is it?" I asked, frightened.

"It's Mommy, dear," my mom said.

"Come in."

My mom opened the door very slowly and saw me holding the dresses.

"Oh, I see you found the dresses Isis left here," she said.

"I didn't know you were home," I said.

"Yes, I am," my mother said.

"These are Isis's dresses?" I asked, looking shocked.

"Yes," she said.

"Are we going to send them back?" I asked.

"She said to keep them," said my mother.

"Can I wear one of them to the dance?" I asked.

"I suppose, dear; they can't fit me," my mother said.

I looked at the dresses, and they were so beautiful. One was red with tons of gems on it. The other was green with diamonds all around the waist. I was so happy that Isis had left me my own tiny mall—the mall that I needed to look my absolute best for this dance. I had to let go of the sadness that there would be no Kingston. I needed to move on and have a good time without him. I tried to think about how good it would be to just go to this party and have a good time. But that was as hard as ever, because I knew that I couldn't fully enjoy myself. The ring gave me more friends in school than I could ever ask for. The bad thing about it was that it couldn't give me true friends like Lennie and Kingston. I felt happy with the ring, but at the same time I felt trapped. Its magic could give me only the bare minimum, not everything.

I wish this could be the end of my story, but unfortunately it isn't. It felt like a never-ending story that I would have to live with. The dance was that night, and I still hadn't picked out a dress. I decided to wear the green dress with diamonds around the waist. I wore a pair of studded diamond shoes that had one-inch heels. I hoped that I would be looked at as the prettiest girl in school, but I felt pretty on the inside and outside already, and that's all that mattered.

I pinned up my hair into a bun-like hairdo. Then I put clips around it. You would have thought I was a princess. My sparkly lip gloss shone like the stars in the sky. My blush made my cheeks so pink and so smooth. I was ready for my freshman dance. The final touch of my outfit was jewels. I wore diamond earrings and a necklace. It matched my entire wardrobe, and I felt like a princess going to the school dance. Last but not least, I had to put on the ring that made this entire life possible for me. I slowly slipped my oval-shaped blue ring onto my index finger. It sort of clashed with the outfit, but I needed it. This ring was going to bring me a lot of luck— all the luck I needed.

The doorbell rang extremely loudly; I could hear it echo around the entire house. I grabbed my matching green clutch and walked out of my room. There Shawn was standing, waiting there for me. It was like a fairytale, only he wasn't my prince.

"Have fun at the dance!" my dad said.

"See you soon," said my mother.

"The limo is outside," said Shawn.

"A limo!" I said in a shocked voice. "I didn't think this was a senior prom."

"No, it was a treat from my dad," Shawn said happily.

I walked toward the limo and reached to open the door. Shawn came right up behind me and opened it for me.

"Thanks," I said. "You are quite the gentleman."

Inside, the limo was spacious, and it had tiny stars on the ceiling. The driver greeted us in a polite manner and then we were on our way. The limo was silent; I didn't know what to say to Shawn. I didn't really know him that well.

"So how are classes?" he asked.

"Good," I said.

"How's life?" he asked.

"Good," I said, looking confused.

We were so bored with one another; we had nothing to chat about. We knew nothing about each other. We never really talked; I just had a crush on him because of how he looked, not who he was as a person. I had picked Shawn for all the wrong reasons. But he was my date for the night, and that was that.

We couldn't pull up to the school fast enough. I was so happy to finally get out of that car. The limo was spacious, yet I still felt invaded. I slowly got out, and Shawn followed me. I didn't want to go anywhere with Shawn. I just walked fast into the gym, where I knew the dance would be.

"What's the rush, Tory?" Shawn asked.

"It's nothing, Shawn," I said, lying to him.

The last thing I wanted to do was make him feel bad. I just wanted the night to go by really fast. I didn't want to be at the freshman formal anymore. Something didn't feel right; it just wasn't a good time to be with Shawn at that moment.

By the time I walked into the gym with Shawn, I was so happy. The gym no longer looked like a gym; it looked like a mansion that was hosting a ball. The lights were dimmed, and the floors sparkled because of the glow above.

"Hey Tory," the ghetto girls said.

"What's up, Shawn," said G-Crew.

The party got a little crazy. Everyone was dancing and having a good time. I was still keeping my distance from my date; I just wanted to dance with all of my friends. I was walking around, and then a slow song came on—a song slow enough to stop the entire dance floor.

"Tory, would you like to dance?" asked Shawn.

"Sure," I said in a small voice.

I couldn't say no; I didn't want him to feel bad. I just wanted the night to be over. But what dance goes by without a slow song? He took my hand and led me to the middle of the dance floor. He started to pull me close to him, but I tried to drift away. We slowly danced to the sound of the music.

"I'm really glad you chose me, Tory," Shawn said.

"Looks like I made a good decision," I said, sounding frustrated.

"You're, like, the most popular girl in school," he said.

"So?" I responded in a perplex voice. Is that the only reason you wanted to take me to the dance?"

"Yes," Shawn said. "Reputation is everything to me."

"Shawn, this dance is over!" I screamed, pushing him back.

The boy I had a crush on didn't really like me for me. He liked only the way I looked and the reputation I had. There was no sign of anything real in our relationship. He loved our status together, not who we were together. I was so angry; this dance had turned into a nightmare. The ring on my finger turned a dark shade of brown. I don't believe the ring could detect how angry I was. I left the dance floor and ran outside. It didn't matter where I was going, as long as I was away from Shawn.

I walked to the back of the schoolyard, where there was a lot of grass. There I walked slowly with my dress dragging through the grass. I was so sad, and just so depressed. The ring couldn't change people's outlooks on certain aspects of life. All it could do was make certain wishes come true. I needed time away from this thing. It seemed like people wanted to be my friend because of the status I had in high school rather than because of who I was—the real Tory that I wanted to show people. I sat on a rock beside a tree, hoping no one would find me. I drifted off into space, looking up at the night sky. I started to count the stars in the sky, but there were just too many to count. After a solid couple of minutes went, by I started to feel at peace.

All of a sudden I heard footsteps coming from behind me. I was scared out of my mind. I didn't know what to do, and I started to worry about who it was. Then around the corner came Kingston. I ran up to him and gave him a huge hug. The stars shone brightly on his face, and the wind blew my hair as I ran to him. I couldn't believe he was standing right in front of me. I thought I was dreaming for a couple of seconds. But I wasn't at all; he was really there.

"Kingston is that you?" I asked, shouting from a distance.

"Yes," he said.

I ran up to him and gave him the biggest hug he could ever imagine. He held me tight in his arms. Tears of joy flowed from my cheeks.

"I can't believe you are here," I said.

"I came to visit; I knew the dance would be tonight," Kingston said. "I wanted to surprise you; people told me you ran out here."

"I was mad that you weren't here," I replied.

"Well, I am here now," he said.

Another slow song started to play in the distance. Kingston and I both could hear it coming from the school.

"One last dance before I go won't hurt," Kingston said.

"It won't," I replied.

He slowly took my hand, and we both danced under the moonlight. It was a dance that is done only in heaven. I was so happy the night ended that way. Nothing mattered anymore, except the sound of the music. I was so happy to see him. Moreover, I was glad the dance ended with me dancing with my best friend. The ring lit up a bright shade of yellow; I was so glad that it wasn't brown. At the end of the dance, I was one happy girl. The best part about this entire dance was that the ring knew I was happy too.

Chapter 19

A Model's Rainbow

The dance was over way too soon, and I was upset that my best friend was gone again. I really enjoyed the dance because of Kingston. I didn't even feel guilty about the way I had treated Shawn. He was the guy that just liked me because of my reputation, and not who I was. I never wanted to speak to him again; I didn't care how pretty his hazel eyes were or how muscular he looked at school. I honestly didn't even remember that I went to the dance with Shawn. All I remembered was dancing under the moonlight with Kingston. Nothing that happened at that dance mattered other than Kingston and me. Unfortunately, it was over. The dance was gone, and it was back to another day of school, along with school-related things I had to catch up on.

I had just started to walk to study hall when I heard someone interrupting my thoughts.

"Hey Tory!" said one of the Quiet Girls.

I hoped whoever was calling me was calling me about something important. I'd had a romantic night with Kingston, and I wasn't going to let anyone mess up my day. I was a young woman who really wanted to end my freshman year of high school peacefully.

"Yes?" I replied.

When I turned around, the entire Quiet Girl clique was behind me, looking right at me. I could even hear them whispering behind my back.

"Did you know you won the queen crown?" said Weddle, one of the Quiet Girls.

"No," I replied, looking shocked.

"You won!" said Weddle, sounding surprised. "You and Shawn won the freshman king and queen crowns! But no one could find you. Where were you?"

"I left early; I was feeling sick," I replied.

I turned around quickly, trying to get to class. I completely ignored the Quiet Girls' voices behind my back. I couldn't believe that I had been nominated and selected as the new queen. I was the freshman queen of the school, and I didn't even know it, as I had been too busy speaking to Kingston. I felt Kingston should have been my king, not Shawn, who had just been using me for my reputation. Queen or no queen, I didn't like the king that was nominated. What a royal pain for a real queen like me.

I walked slowly into my study hall classroom. I just wanted to study for the finals that were soon approaching. Every time I heard the word "finals," I felt as if I were sitting in a movie theater while a preview played really loudly. But the announcement of finals sounded like a horror movie to me. My thoughts were interrupted by footsteps. I sat down at my desk, and Shawn came right up behind me.

"Hi, Tory, this is for you," he said with attitude in his voice. Shawn dropped the crown on the desk in front of me. It was a beautiful silver crown, made perfectly for a royal with lovely diamonds going around it. I couldn't even look directly at it, as the diamonds were shining so brightly in my eyes. "It would have gone perfectly with your dress," said Shawn.

I didn't respond to his attitude at all. I was way too upset with Shawn to even give him the time of day. He had really hurt me, and I didn't want to speak to him at all.

"You left me up on that stage with the crown alone," he said.

"I know I did," I replied.

"I know you're mad at me," Shawn said.

"I'm glad you know," I said, responding with bitter sass.

Shawn walked away without even looking back at me. I know the ring decreased the drama in my life, but one thing I didn't want was a false friend around me. And that's exactly what Shawn was. He was not a good friend; nor was he the boyfriend I would want to have in my life.

I turned my back and started to study my work. I wasn't going to let any distractions get in my way. As I started to write, trying to complete my work, I was sadly distracted by the ring's strange color changes. It was so odd what was happening. The color of the ring changed drastically before my eyes. The ring cycled through blue, red, brown, and black, and then it turned purple. *But what does this color mean?* I thought to myself, wondering what the color of the ring meant. I wanted to know so deeply, but the ring had no writing on it, as it had when it was orange. I should have asked Isis the crazy rules of this ring. Now I was stuck wondering what each color meant. I wasn't in the mood for any more surprises in my freshman year. The only thing I wanted was to end my high school year with no drama. Whatever purple meant, I just hoped it meant something good.

While I was sitting down doing my work, distracted by the ring's purplish color, I kept losing more focus because the ring was turning so purple. I got a little nervous at first, but what could I do? Then I started to hear more whispers behind my back about the modeling auditions, which were next period. The seniors would be the judge of who would be in the big show. Unfortunately, I was one of the girls auditioning. Every girl in school was talking about doing it and winning it for the money. As for me, I just wanted to do it for fun, because modeling was something I had always wanted to try. What can I say, I thought it might boost my confidence. I feel that models have a lot of confidence—something I had never had much of. I thought, *How bad it could hurt to be a part of a modeling show?*

The auditions were just minutes away, and I was already feeling anxious. The ring was still purple—really purple. I hoped this didn't mean anything bad; I just wished the ring would get me through this audition.

The bell rang extremely loudly in my ears, which meant it was time for my next class. But there was no class for me, just an audition that I was scared to try out for. As I walked through the halls, I could hear the ghetto girls' loud voices. I wasn't in the mood to hear them at that moment. I just wanted to get through this audition in peace. The ghetto girls were on their way to the audition as well. The audition was going to be one big school experience, and some were in it for the money, while I was in it to become a better me.

When the time for the audition arrived, every female in the school was lined up to audition. I was so nervous I felt I couldn't compete with all of these girls. I just wanted to run away and hide for a while. But that was what the old Tory would have done, not the new Tory. I stood in a line full of girls for about an hour. Soon I was standing in front of the senior judges. That's when my heart started beating fast. You would have thought the audition was for Miss America.

Then came the moment when I was stared at by the entire school. I had been humiliated so many times in my life that it didn't matter to me if it happened again. Before I knew it, the music came on really loudly. All eyes were still on me, but I was the only person being stared at. I strutted down that runway as if I were a professional. I could hear the ghetto girls giggling behind my back, but none of that mattered. The sound of the music took over. No longer was I Tory; I was supermodel Tory. When I hit the bottom of the stage, I blew a kiss at the judges. I showed how proud I was of myself. Many clapped loudly, and the seniors smiled and giggled.

When it was time for the Judges to decide who they wanted, I didn't know if I was going to be picked or if I was just a girl being laughed at. They started to call names one by one. As for me, I didn't even know whom I was competing against. I honestly blocked out the entire show. I wanted it to be over; I just wanted to go home. I wasn't the kind of girl that liked a lot of attention. As they announced the names, I heard "Tory Morton." I had been selected.

I was in awe. I had never auditioned for anything in my life. I'd always thought I would lose. I made myself a sore loser all of the time before I even gave myself a real chance. I was officially part of the modeling team. I was going to be in the school fashion show, and the best part was that I had a great shot at the award. The show was a couple of days away, and I would have to constantly rehearse. I was happy to be a part of this; the ring was making the unthinkable come true. I can't say this wasn't a happy moment.

The seniors led the selected girls into a big classroom where we chose from a list of dresses to wear to the fashion show. I was just glad that I didn't have to worry about buying anything or begging Isis for anything. I didn't feel comfortable wearing Isis's dresses that she had left around anyway. The dresses were hung all around the history classroom. It was like a mini mall for all of us girls. We ran around the classroom, picking out the dress we felt would look good on us. The seniors wanted us to pick out the dress we liked best so we could get measured and have it sized to the way it fit. The best part was that we got to keep the dress we picked out.

I was so happy to finally be participating in this. I was so surprised I even got picked to be in this show. All I was looking forward to doing at that moment was finding the perfect dress. I looked down and saw a long dress with diamonds up the side. The dress was beautiful I just couldn't stop looking at it. It was a baby blue dress that shone at the side because of the diamonds. I grabbed it before anyone else could. Then I ran to the bathroom to change into it. I didn't even want to wait to get measured. I just tried it on, and it was perfect. This dress was the perfect fit for me. I let my hair down and kept looking at myself in the mirror. *This is what a true beauty queen looks like.* I looked down at the ring and saw it was turning many different colors.

"Oh no," I said.

I didn't know what to do. I thought I had seen the ring turn every color it could. But now there were just so many colors. I hoped it meant something good. But what could I do? I looked in the mirror not paying the ring any mind. This ring was starting to scare me. Whatever the rainbow of colors meant, I didn't want to know, because I didn't have a good feeling about it at all. I walked out the restroom and went into the room where all the girls were trying on dresses. When I closed the door behind me, everyone turned and looked at me; then everything went completely quiet.

"Tory, you look so great!" shouted a senior girl.

Everyone crowded around me, and there was a chaos of compliments. No one looked as good as in her dress as I did. Compared to everyone in that room, I was Cinderella.

"Line up for rehearsal; the show will be approaching soon," said a senior.

All of us were lined up by height, and we rehearsed in the long school hallway. All of us rehearsed until everything was perfect. The ring was still shining in many weird rainbow colors. I missed it being just an orange shade; that was so much easier to understand.

After rehearsal was over, we sat down for a meeting about what the big show would be like. "The show is in three days, and we are so happy that you guys are our models," a senior announced. "There is a huge award of money, along with pictures in the school magazine, if you are the winner. We are so happy to finally come to this day where we can share fashion glory with our school. Please remember this isn't about winning the prize; it's about being a part of a team, a modeling team. The show will be hosted in a big assembly in front of the whole student body. Your names will be screamed out, and you are expected to look your best. Please have your dress fitted and cleaned. Your hair and makeup team will be in room 203 upstairs in the school. Dress to impress, and model for fun, not the prize!"

The ring was still turning rainbow colors, and it wasn't showing any sign of stopping. Unfortunately, I could barely focus on what the senior was saying because of this.

"Wow, what a beautiful ring!" A junior girl said.

"Thanks," I replied quickly, hoping that she wouldn't say anything else about the ring. But of course she just had to keep going with the conversation, and trying to touch it while it was turning one hundred different colors.

The girl moved to slowly touch the ring, and it glowed really brightly. *Zap!* The ring shocked her hands; you would have thought it had electrocuted her.

"Aah!" the junior screamed loudly in excruciating pain.

"I didn't know what to do; I hadn't known it was going to shock her. Isis had never told me not to let anyone touch the ring. If she had, I certainly didn't remember.

All of the girls turned around and looked at the junior girl. But I felt they were staring more at me than anything.

"What happened?" asked a senior, looking scared.

"Tory's rainbow ring just shocked me!" the junior girl shouted.

My heart started to beat as fast as it could ever go. I was scared, and all eyes in the room were on me. I couldn't help but just make it look like a freak accident.

"I have no idea how that happened," I said, looking as perplexed as everyone else in the room.

"Well the show is in three days, so let's get back to work," said the senior.

I was the happiest woman on earth when she said that sentence. I didn't want anyone in the school to know that my ring had magic powers. I knew that if anyone found out about this, I would be in big trouble; everyone would want to steal it from me. I wished the ring would stop changing colors, but it wouldn't. I also wished the ring had not shocked this innocent girl. Unfortunately, I had no say in what the ring did; it had a huge rainbow mind of its own. The entire meeting was interrupted by the principal's deep voice over the loudspeaker.

"The modeling show will be pushed back to the end of the school year. Everyone should be more focused on passing finals then anything else."

Oh no! I thought. Now the show wasn't going to be anytime soon.

"The show will occur at the end-of-year school celebration," said the principal.

Everyone was so upset that the show had been moved to a different date. All of the students had talents they wanted to show at the end of the school year. From what I heard around the halls, G-Crew was going to show off their new rap thing. But maybe not, because I had also heard they were in some police trouble at the moment. As for the ghetto girls, they were going to be in the show and show off their new dance moves. I also heard the Quiet Girls were going to demonstrate how to meditate. I guess that's why we called them the Quiet Girls.

It took me forever to get over the fact that the show wouldn't be for a while.

I just wanted to get it over with. It was like one of those feelings when you have to make a public speech but you don't want to because your heart is skipping so many beats.

Finals were slowly approaching, and it didn't take me long to realize that the principal was right; I hadn't focused on studying like I should have. If I wanted to pass ninth grade, I would have to pass my finals. I walked to my locker and looked at all of the books in it. *How on earth will I pass my finals?* I had no confidence in my own abilities. The ring started to change many different colors again.

After school was out, I went straight to my bedroom to study. I locked myself in there, studying all that I could. When I stopped studying, I looked up at the ring. I was almost falling asleep, and ready to give up . The ring was a light shade of blue. Then it started to look really watery. The ring looked like some sort of a portal that could harm me. My finger started to shake, and the ring strapped tightly around my hand. Words that looked like they were floating appeared: "Have confidence in you, and you will succeed." I couldn't believe the ring was speaking to me.

"But how?" I replied.

I couldn't believe I was speaking to a piece of jewelry. But it was speaking to me, so why couldn't I question it back?

"Who are you speaking to, Tory?" my mom asked.

My mother opened my room door as usual, interrupting and asking many questions.

"The ring," I replied.

"The ring?" she said, sounding perplexed.

"I mean no one," I said very quickly.

"Tory, dinner is ready, honey!" she said. She walked away whispering to herself, "Finals have made my daughter a little crazy,"

After dinner was over, I ran back upstairs to complete my finals studies. I thought, *If the ring can believe in me, I should be able to believe in myself.* I made a study chart for myself, and then I studied every little bit of vocabulary that I could. I knew I could do this; it was just a matter of me believing that I could. I couldn't depend on the ring for everything.

The next morning, I felt more than ready for my finals. I just knew that I would get an A on every single final that I had, because of the work I had put in. My first final was in English, which I was on my way to passing. Everyone sat down and prepared to take the test. Before I put my pencil to my paper, G-Crew walked into English class. I guess they were out of jail. At least the rumor was they had been in jail. Koury sat down next to me and smiled.

"Where were you guys?" I asked, looking really concerned.

Truth be told, I wasn't concerned—just nosy.

"We got suspended for a couple of days for pilfering from the store down the street," he replied.

"Are the rumors true? Did you go to prison?" I asked.

"Luckily no, they gave us a break," he replied.

All I could focus on was passing my final. I started to work on it, but I was interrupted by a voice.

"Wow! Look at that ring; it's shining gold," Koury said really loudly.

He tried to touch my ring with his fingers. I couldn't stop him quickly enough. *Zap!* The ring shocked him. He screamed extremely loudly in excruciating pain.

"What is the problem?" said Mrs. Ma-Donny.

"Tory's bling shocked me," said Koury.

I was too scared to deny it or say anything at all. I just stood there looking at the ring in disappointment.

"Rings don't bite, Koury," said Mrs. Ma-Donny.

"I have to focus on my exam," Glow said.

"Me too," I replied.

Everyone was looking at me and Koury. The entire class was completely distracted.

"I'm not touching no more jewels on you," said Koury.

"That would probably be a good thing," I responded with a bit of attitude.

I focused all day on passing my final. The ring continued to glow gold. During the final I wondered what it meant, but I didn't focus on it. I just knew that it had shocked Koury unexpectedly.

All day, I couldn't think of anything but all the tests I had in all my classes. When the day was over, I could finally breathe.

I was walking down the spiral staircase when I saw Koury give me a dirty look. I put my hand up so he could see the ring.

"Aah!" Koury screamed, and he ran down the spiral stairs.

I guess he won't be touching my jewelry anymore.

My finals were over, and all I had to tackle was the modeling show, which would have been on that very day had it not been moved to the end-of-the-school-year celebration. I didn't know what was going to happen, but I needed to keep my focus.

"Congrats on completing all of your finals," the principal announced. "We will see you tomorrow, on the last day of school, when we will celebrate the end of the school year! Report cards and final grades will be mailed, and you will find out whether you will have to repeat a grade or class. Have a great summer!"

The entire school cheered and left the school in a hurry. Everyone was so happy to have made it to the end of the school year.

I walked out of school thinking about nothing but the show. I was always caught up in my own world when I had to focus on myself. I thought that since my finals had ended early, I should spend the day pampering myself, and that's exactly what I did.

First, I went to the hairstylist and had my hair done just like a hairdo I saw in a magazine. Then I got my nails done at a small place in town. I knew I would be the belle of the ball, and I loved the way I was looking. When I got home, the ring was still shining gold. I was so happy, I didn't exactly know what gold meant, but, it must have meant "Do well on your final, and then pamper yourself." That's exactly what I did.

***

The next day, it was time for the big show. I was so happy it was finally here. I was dressed up, and I looked like a princess to be. Everyone was sitting in the audience. I was so scared of what might happen next. I hoped and prayed that I wouldn't fall on the stage or trip on anyone. I thought, *Maybe I should have rehearsed more instead of pampering myself.*

"I love your dress, Tory," a girl behind me said.

"Thanks," I replied.

Then I heard her whisper behind my back.

"I would so look better in that dress," she whispered to a girl in a white dress.

I didn't know why girls got so catty when it came to modeling shows. I just needed to keep my focus on being the winner. Even if I didn't win, at least I would put forth the effort.

Before I knew it, I was backstage with tons of girls. There were other performers too. G-Crew did their rap thing. The quiet girls showed everyone how to meditate. The Exclusive Clique even did a dance. They were all good performances. But at the end-of-school celebration, the modeling show was the closing show.

One of the senior girls lined us up by height. I was one of the tallest girls, so I had to go last. I was so upset that I had to go last. I didn't want to go last and be the last one being stared at. I quickly took many deep breaths. I felt dizzy. All I could look at was the ring. It started to shine crazy rainbow colors again. I just kept taking deep breaths.

Soon it was my turn to come out. I stepped out slowly, and the wind blew my hair. The lights flashed in my eyes, very bright. I started to walk, and the crowd screamed and cheered me on. It seemed they were cheering for everyone, but they cheered louder for me. I walked out, strutting down that runway as if I owned it. The judges were pleased at the way I looked. They smiled back at me. When I got to the end of the stage, I winked my right eye. The judges laughed and were pleased at the way I handled the runway, so confident and firm. I was a model in everyone's eyes, but I was a diamond in my own eyes.

At the end of the show, all of the girls lined up on the stage. The platform felt as if it were shaking because everyone wanted to be the winning girl.

"After two hundred ten votes from the student body, the winner is Victoria Morton." the speaker announced.

I had never been so happy to hear my full name. The crowd roared. I was the winner. The Exclusive Clique passed me my roses and a crown.

"You have also won the seven-hundred-dollar award, and you will be in the school magazine," announced the speaker.

I was so happy, and I felt like the celebrity I had always wanted to be. People were chasing me around the school, wanting to take pictures with me . It was just like the dream I'd had that I thought was a nightmare. But it wasn't a nightmare; it was a dream come true.

I am glad this happened to me. I am glad I gave myself the chance for it to happen to me! My miserable freshman year was over, and it ended with a sweet story to pass on.

Chapter 20

The Vacation

My freshman year of high school was finally over. I couldn't believe everything I had learned during just one year of high school. I also couldn't believe the crazy ride I had been through with the ring. I also enjoyed the last couple of days of school. I got more good-bye hugs than nasty comments. That would have never happened without the ring. As for the ring, it went back to its original color—blue. I got home early from school, and yes, I was happy my parents weren't home yet. I put my bag down and saw a postcard on the floor. On the postcard was a picture of a beautiful beach that said "Bahamas" on it. The picture also had a huge cruise ship floating away toward the horizon. I thought, *What a nice little vacation spot.* A vacation was what I felt I needed after dealing with a high school nightmare and the ring. I turned the postcard over and saw what it stated:

Hello, Tory! I hope things are going well with the ring. The school year is over! I hope you enjoyed your time with it. By the way, I can't wait for our family vacation in the Bahamas. See you then!

Love,

Isis Fierce

I was so shocked about the postcard that I almost screamed. A nice trip to the Bahamas with Isis was just what I needed. What a pleasant surprise, and what a secret that had been kept from me. I ran upstairs to start packing for the big family trip!

What a wonderful end-of-the-year surprise to have! I needed a vacation. It would be nice to see Isis again. But even though I was surprised, I wondered if Isis would take the ring back. I wouldn't mind giving her the ring back; it was hers to begin with. But I loved having the ring on my finger, changing my life. In my room I saw a letter from school on my bed. They had mailed my report card to my home. I couldn't believe it; I had passed all of my finals. I also had been promoted to the next grade. There were straight As on the report card. I wondered what my sophomore year would be like.

Three days went by, and all I could do was think about my big vacation. When it was time to leave, I was more than happy about it! I couldn't wait to get on the cruise ship and sail far away. When the limo that Isis's parents had sent for my family and me pulled up, all I could do was look crazily shocked.

We drove for about five hours to get to the ship. I couldn't complain; it was a comfortable ride in the limo. When we pulled up to the cruise ship, I was amazed at the way it looked. Angel and Isaac ran up to hug me, and so did Isis's entire family.

Isis grabbed me by the hand and took me outside to the deck. Farther down the boat were some huge flights of stairs. The sun was still a little bright, and it was setting really slowly. I walked up the flight of high stairs with Isis. I was a little nervous about what she was going to show me, but what could I do? I just had to expect that she might ask for the ring back.

Isis took me to the top of the ship, where there was a much better view of the sunset.

"So how do you like the view?" she asked.

"Remarkable!" I replied.

"How has the ring been treating you?" she asked.

I got scared and started to shake a little bit. I didn't want to answer her, but I had to. I couldn't just stand there looking crazy. Isis gave me a look that said, "You'd better answer me."

"The ring has treated me very well," I said.

"You thought I would forget about it, didn't you?" she asked.

"I can't lie; I really did," I responded slowly.

I didn't know what else to say to Isis. If I gave the ring back, my life would probably go back to misery. If I kept the ring, my life would probably be perfect forever. I was just going to ask her what I needed to. I didn't care at that moment what she thought. Why did I need to beat around the bush?

"Do you want the ring back?" I asked.

"No," said Isis.

I was so happy when she said no, because her life was already perfect and she didn't need the ring like I did. But who was I to judge? It wasn't my ring in the first place.

"Why not? It can work so many miracles," I said.

"For those who need the miracles," she responded. "There was a time I felt my life was turned upside down, and then I found the ring and it changed me," Isis said.

"Were all of your experiences like mine?" I asked.

I wanted to ask Isis a hundred questions, but I still didn't want to seem nosy. I even wanted to tell her about my experiences with the ring. But what would she say? What would she do?

"Tory, I don't know what your experiences were like, and I'm not supposed to," she said.

"Why not?" I asked.

"Everyone's experience with the ring is different, but it should be kept sacred and secretive," Isis said. "If you speak about it to anyone you're not going to pass it on to, it will immediately lose its power. That's why I told you not to tell anyone about it, remember? So I guess it kept its power and kept taking care of you."

I looked at the ring and began to admire its blue shine. I was so happy it was still on my finger and Isis hadn't taken it away.

"Tory, you can't have the ring forever?" Isis said.

"Why not? You just said you didn't want it back," I said with a sassy attitude.

"It's not meant for you to have forever. When you need it, it will glow and help you, with the word 'swoop'; but when you don't need it anymore, it will turn purple."

"So its magic isn't going to last forever?" I asked.

"No. Nothing lasts forever," she responded. "The ring's power can be used only for a certain amount of time. Then you must pass it on to someone who really needs it.

"Who needs it next? Who needs it more than I do?" I asked with anger in my voice. I was so upset that I had to let go of the ring that had given me such a happy ending to high school.

"I don't want to give up the ring and have high school go back to the bad way it used to be," I said.

I could hear the distress in my voice; I knew I was going to cry eventually.

"You see, Tory, that was what it was supposed to do for you," Isis said, looking at me.

"Make my high school a wonderful dream?" I asked.

"No, give you the confidence you needed to succeed!" she said.

"High school didn't have to remain a bad nightmare like you were making it; you made it that way because you thought it would be easier that way." Isis said.

"I did?" I said with sadness in my voice.

"You did," she said. "You thought you couldn't give yourself a chance or take a risk to try anything; you gave up on yourself before you even gave yourself a chance."

I knew everything Isis was saying was the truth. I couldn't even deny it and say she was wrong.

"All that the ring did for you, you could have done yourself," Isis said.

"I am not sure of that," I said.

"There you go doubting yourself again," she said.

I looked down at the ring, knowing she was absolutely right. Maybe high school wouldn't have been the nightmare I thought it would be. I had never given myself a real chance; I isolated myself from everyone I knew.

"What about the bullies?" I asked.

"You let them bully you. You could have stood up to them a long time ago," she said. The ring gave you a backbone that you needed, but yet you always had it. Have confidence in yourself, believe in yourself, and prosper for yourself. Tory, you are so much more than you give yourself credit for." She smiled at me.

My face got really red, and I started to cry. I knew exactly what Isis was talking about. Why did I need this ring to show me this? I couldn't believe I never had the confidence to do the things I had accomplished with the ring.

Isis put her hand on my shoulder. "You are so much more powerful without the ring," she whispered in my ear.

"So what do I do now?" I asked.

"You take the ring and pass it down to someone that needs it," she said.

"I don't know anyone," I replied.

"Well then, you must get rid of it for someone else to use it," she said.

"It's going to lose its power very shortly, Tory," Isis said.

The ring started to shake on my hand. It turned a shade of dark purple. I didn't know what was happening. The sun had set, and the stars filled the night sky. My hand was still shaking with the ring on my finger. It started to glow many different colors. It was glowing all of the colors it had been throughout high school: yellow, red, orange, blue, and then a dark shade of purple. Isis was standing there watching as the ring shook on my hand, turning purple. Before I knew it, the ring turned red and started to burn my hand. The burning felt as if my hand were on a hot stove for about three whole minutes. It became so painful I took the ring off and threw it, and it flew right into the ocean, flashing red as it fell.

"Nooooo!" I shouted.

The ring was gone forever. It could have been anywhere in the ocean.

"Isis, what are we going to do?" I said.

Isis was as cool as a cucumber. She said absolutely nothing but just stared at the ocean. I wondered if she was going to be mad at me. I had thrown the ring she gave me right into the ocean. I hoped she wasn't mad at me. I was shaking as I imagined what she was going to say.

"It's okay, Tory. The ring has no use for you or me anymore," she said. It's gone forever now, and none of us will see it again."

"Why did it hurt my hand like that?" I asked. My hand was still really red from the burning sensation.

"You were having some trouble letting it go," she responded. "As a result, it helped you let it go."

I looked at the stars and then the ocean. The ocean appeared to be a shade of red because the ring's power was shining under the water. I wanted to cry; there was still a huge indentation on my finger where the ring once was.

"I hope whoever finds it next is blessed just like we were," Isis said.

I was so sad and so upset, and I was crying my eyes out. I felt I needed that ring more than anything.

"Isis, how will they know the incantation, or all they need to know?" I asked, looking perplexed.

"They can make up their own or just use its magic," she said.

Isis made me want to slap her. After all the ring had done for her and me, all she could do was just stand there and show no emotion.

I was so upset that I couldn't keep the ring, I ran down the stairs and onto the deck. I looked down at the ocean, but all I saw were waves on the water. I cried, hoping the ring would come back to me. One of my tears fell in the ocean. I knew at that moment that the ring was gone forever. But Isis still showed no emotion.

"What happens now?" I asked, still looking very sad.

"I don't know what will happen. The ring will find its next person to help somehow," she said.

"Who—a whale or a fish?" I asked sarcastically.

Isis laughed loudly, and I started to laugh too. I was so upset; I didn't know how this could have happened. I was without the piece of jewelry that changed my life.

"I know you have grown attached, but the ring can no longer help you," said Isis. "It taught you all you needed to know," she said.

"Easy for you to say, Isis," I replied with a sassy attitude. "You have everything."

"Yeah, I do," she said. "The ring did make me kind of cocky. And it made you more confident."

"I guess," I replied.

Immediately my sadness was gone. I finally realized why Isis was acting the way she was. She had passed this ring on to me because she felt that I needed it. But when it was time for me to pass it on, I unfortunately didn't want to. So the ring made me give it up.

Isis walked beside me and put her hand on my shoulder. "I am sorry I didn't tell you all you needed to know about the ring, but I thought it would be more beneficial for you to learn about it by yourself," she said.

"I am so happy you let me learn about it," I responded with a sad voice.

Isis grabbed my hand and walked me back up the stairs. On the very far end of the deck upstairs were two brown hammocks. We both lay on the hammocks, swinging back and forth. We looked at the stars and the moon, which were shining so brightly. This was just beginning to become a nice vacation. Isis knew exactly the words to say to make me calm. We rocked back and forth on the hammocks.

"I am glad it was you that I passed the ring down to," Isis said.

"Why is that?" I asked, looking perplexed.

"The way you handled it and took care of it and kept the secret," she said. "I am also glad you are my cousin; it's nice to have someone in the family to speak with," she said.

"Thanks, Isis," I replied. "I'm happy you're my cousin too."

We held hands, looking up at the stars, swinging back and forth on the hammocks. All night we just whispered and whispered about the ring. Isis even laughed about the silly stories

I told her about the Hulk and my teachers. I looked up at the sky and saw a shooting star that shot right by.

"Make a wish," Isis said insistently.

"Without the ring," I said sassily.

We both laughed and spoke about how we missed the ring .

"I wish the ring will go to someone who really needs it, since I didn't get a chance to pass it on," I said in a whisper to myself. I closed my eyes really tightly and hoped my wish would come true.

Isis and I couldn't stop chatting about what we were going to do on the rest of our vacation.

I realized at that moment of letting the ring go that the ring wasn't there to make miracles happen; it was there to teach me. It was there to guide me. If I had more confidence in myself, things probably would have turned out differently in high school.

I guess I had all the power that I needed without the ring; I was just too stubborn to realize it, and too blind to notice. The ring wasn't only a piece of jewelry; it was a message to my life.

Thank you, ring!

128

Epilogue

The ring sits at the bottom of the ocean, still glowing purple. Then it starts to glow tons of different colors. A fish swims by it and swims around it for a couple of seconds. Then the waves become heavier, eventually pushing the glowing ring to the seashore. The ring is pushed onto the seaside, where there is a ton of sand. There are people on the beach, lying down to get tan. A homeless man who smells and looks dirty sits by the seashore. He notices the ring to the right of his foot. He slowly picks it up, studying what it is. The ring glows the color of bright blue. He puts the ring on his index finger, but it doesn't fit. So instead he puts it on his thumb, where it fits perfectly. He walks down the beach with the ring glowing different colors. He stops and finds a piece of paper on the ground. He picks it up and reads it closely. To his left, two boys are listening to the radio and tanning on the beach. The paper the homeless man looks at is a lottery ticket. He sees the following numbers on the ticket: 8, 5, 6, 2, 1.

A radio is playing very loudly on the beach; he can hear everything clearly.

"The winning numbers of the lottery today are eight, five, six, two, one," says the radio. "Come collect your prize of seven million dollars."

The homeless man smiles to himself. He jumps up and down, so happy, screaming with joy. The ring is shining the color yellow, and he is screaming about how rich he is.

"I won the lottery!" he says.

It is unfortunate the homeless man doesn't know the exact rules of the ring. Rule number one is that you don't tell anyone what the ring has given you, and you don't shout it out.

The entire beach can hear him screaming and looks over at the man, whom they never before paid any attention to. Soon the entire beach is running after the homeless man for the winning ticket!

About the Author

I hope you enjoy the wonderful journey of Tory's high school life with a magical ring. I wrote this book when I was in high school. It was a joy to get into my creative imagination and bring it to life with this book. I started writing books when I was eleven years old. As a young girl I had such a creative imagination. When I wrote, I felt as if my world of fantasy were coming to life. I have always wanted to be an author. I am so glad and thankful that I have the opportunity to finally call myself one as I publish my first book. If there is one thing that I have learned from my story, it is to believe in yourself, because you have no idea where your life will take you. My writing has made me stronger as a person. I have learned so much in this one little story that is just a fantasy. I hope to share this adventure of Tory with others to help them laugh, learn, and be inspired.

Enjoy!

CPSIA information can be obtained at www.ICGtesting.com
Printed in the USA
LVOW05s1213190815

450726LV00022B/238/P